The Bridge to Nowhere

A Richard Jackson Book

The Bridge to Nowhere

Megan McDonald

Orchard Books **|** *New York*

My deep thanks to The Society of Children's Book Writers and Judy Blume for
The Work-in-Progress Grant for Contemporary Fiction; to Rick Sebak, Drew
Nelson, and Al Curry, for research; to Adams Memorial Library, for patience; to
Judi Ingram Adkins, for childhood; to Cathy Camper, for gingerbread pancakes;
to Richard, for light and dark; to my sisters, Susan, Deborah, Michele, and
Melissa, for remembering; and most gratefully to Richard Jackson, for believing.

On page 13, the lines from "April Rain Song" from *The Dream Keeper and
Other Poems* by Langston Hughes, copyright 1932 by Alfred A. Knopf, Inc., and
renewed 1960 by Langston Hughes, are reprinted by permission of the publisher
and Harold Ober Associates Incorporated.
On page 87, the information on rabies is excerpted from *The World Book
Encyclopedia*, © 1992 World Book, Inc., and appears by permission of the
publisher.
On page 98, the lines from "You Ain't Goin' Nowhere," copyright © 1967, 1973 by
Dwarf Music, all rights reserved, are used by permission. Written by Bob Dylan.

The article that appears on pages 124–125 is based on an actual newspaper
account of the incident from the *Pittsburgh Post Gazette*, Monday, December
14, 1964.

Orchard Books, 95 Madison Avenue, New York, NY 10016

Manufactured in the United States of America
Book design by Mina Greenstein
The text of this book is set in 12 point Caledonia.
10 9 8 7 6 5 4 3 2 1

Library of Congress Cataloging-in-Publication Data
McDonald, Megan. The bridge to nowhere / by Megan
McDonald.   p.   cm. "A Richard Jackson book"—Half-title.
Summary: Seventh grader Hallie is adjusting to friendship
with an exciting older boy when her father, a bridge builder
temporarily out of work, becomes an angry stranger in his
own house.
ISBN 0-531-05478-0   ISBN 0-531-08628-3 (lib. bdg.)
[1. Fathers and daughters—Fiction. 2. Emotional prob-
lems—Fiction.] I. Title. PZ7.M478419Br 1993
[Fic]—dc20   92-50844

In memory of
MARY LOUISE MCDONALD,
who first inspired the stories,
and
JOHN MCDONALD,
forever building bridges

THE SAXOPHONE PLAYER *eased out a last long, lonely note. It hung in the air and trembled there, vibrating. He came often to practice by the river, beneath the bridge. Maybe it was the sound, the way one note bounced off the steel beams, fractured, became a symphony. Or maybe it was the serenity.*

No traffic here. No roar of engines, whoosh of tires. No horns honking, brakes screeching to a halt. Only the echoes of ironworkers, men who walked the planks, welded steel, tossed rivets, told jokes, and traded stories. Men who one day, one day like any other day, were told to quit work and go home.

They took off their hard hats, wiped the sweat from their brows, and laid down their gloves, never dreaming it would be for the last time.

One man walked out to the end of the bridge, stood at the edge, and, shielding his eyes, looked across to the opposite shore. Or did he look at the river?

Now no one crosses this bridge. For years it has stood unfinished, a silent steel sculpture like a sentence half-spoken, dangling in midair. An arm without fingers.

The Bridge to Nowhere.

1

"Get in the car, Hallie," her mother said in a voice that excluded all possibility of argument. "Don't even dump your schoolbooks. We haven't time."

"Why aren't you at work, Mom?" Hallie asked.

"Get-in-the-car."

Shoulders hunched, her mother clenched the steering wheel with both hands and peered through the windshield, as if driving in a downpour. Except for one thing—no rain. She was muttering, "That man," and "Once and for all. . . ." Hallie didn't feel obliged to listen. She paid little attention until her father's beat-up old junker, stopped at the intersection just ahead, caught her eye. "Hey, there's Dad." Instinctively, she cranked down her window partway.

"Hallie! Roll up that window. I don't want him to see us."

"You mean we're tailing him? I can't believe it, Mom. You're making me follow my own father? Where is it you think he's going?"

"I don't know, but I intend to find out."

They kept at least two cars behind, running three yellow lights on McKnight Road. "Just keep your eye on him, Hallie, while I drive. Don't let him turn. Tell me the second you see his blinker."

"Mom, left! Make a left." In spite of herself, Hallie was momentarily swept up in the chase. "There he goes!"

She lost sight of the car around a bend on Ohio River Boulevard. "Mom, this is crazy. He could just be going to the hardware store, you know. Or maybe picking up that part for the refrigerator you've been bugging him about."

"Not every single day at the same time."

"How on earth do you know that?"

"Ruthie told me. She thought he had a job again because she sees him leave the house every day at three o'clock."

"Mom, how can you believe *her*? She's the biggest busybody in Allegheny County. You're the one who says she never has anything better to do than stand guard behind the curtains all day."

"Now, Hallie . . ."

"Well, I don't see why you have to drag me along. Just because you're into spying doesn't mean I am." Hallie did not want to find out where her father was going. Imagining, for her, was less fearsome than knowing.

They were crossing the Sixth Street Bridge now. A block ahead of them, her father's car pulled up outside a run-down box of a building with neon signs that flashed IRON CITY in the window. The Sparkle Café.

"Turn around, Mom, please. He's probably just meeting one of his old ironworker buddies. Like maybe Porkchop Smitty. Why don't we go home?"

"Shhh."

As if my not talking would allow her to see better. Hallie sighed.

A hand-crayoned shirt cardboard in the window read HELP WANTED in uneven letters. ASK INSIDE.

"Mother. The sign says 'help wanted.' Maybe they need a cook or something, and Dad's thinking about a job. Now, please . . . let's go home before he catches us."

"Wait right here, Hallie," her mother instructed, pulling the car off to the side. "Watch the car while I—"

"First you make me come with you! Now I have to wait here?" Hallie protested, but it was no use pleading. Her mother had already crossed the street.

Hallie leaned on the dashboard until it creased her forehead. Would her mother just stand by the door, waiting? How long would her father be? Restless, she considered pulling out her notebook, starting her homework. A poem. About spring. She dreaded the thought. Would he come out alone? When she looked up, Hallie saw that her father had not gone inside at all. Up ahead, she could see him crossing the street against traffic.

Despite her mother's warning, she left the car and clambered up the steel stairs onto the Sixth Street

Bridge. A blustery wind whipped and knotted her hair. The roar of traffic nearly muffled the tiny chirping of birds, the tinkling of a dog's collar.

Her mother ran alongside the river below, shouting to her father through cupped hands, her dress curtsying in the wind. Unhearing, her father gripped the steel beams of the next bridge upriver. He stepped on the rivet heads, first one foot, then the other. Hallie watched him shinning up the side and over the rail as easily as a squirrel climbing a tree. He leaned over the handrail, staring down into the water.

Two years. Two winters, two summers, and a string of other jobs since work on the bridge had been halted. Yet still it coaxed her father back, the way a long-empty battlefield coaxes back a soldier.

When her sister, Shelley, left for college, she'd been angry with her father for not having a job. And for not seeking one. It meant staying home for her first semester, working at Borden Burger to save money.

"Nobody starts college halfway through freshman year, Dad," Shelley had informed him. "I might as well not go. I won't have any friends."

"Then wait till next year," her father had said, which only made Shelley more determined than ever to leave.

When she did, everything changed. In the three months since, Hallie's father had become a stranger to her. Or so it seemed, now that Shelley was gone.

A lone sea gull gave a piercing cry and swooped low, not far from her father's head. A small tug glided past, pushing a single barge of coal. Two people sat on the river wall, nestled into each other like roosting pigeons. Everywhere around her, the river was full of movement and life. But for her father, she knew, there was nothing except the silent spans of steel, motionless barges piled high with debris, ghosts of cranes, quieter still.

All he cared about was his precious bridge. *Half a bridge, really.* Tears brimmed like hot wax, spilled down Hallie's face. Her vision blurred, but for a split second before she blinked, she could see clearly through the prism of stinging tears: her father, silhouetted against the sky, more shadow than man.

Hallie hugged her sweatshirt to her. Despite the coming of spring, a damp chill penetrated to her skin. She felt paper-thin, as fragile as a wasp's nest left to the wind.

2

"You're kidding! Didn't he know you were following him?" Jude asked, after Hallie burst out with the story. "I mean, what if he saw you?"

"That's what I said to Mom," Hallie said. "I guess I'll find out soon as he gets home."

The two sat facing each other, cross-legged on Jude's bed, as they'd done since second grade.

"If he just goes downtown and hangs out around the Bridge to Nowhere, what's so bad about that? Maybe he likes taking walks by the river," Jude said. "Where did your mom think he was going?"

"I'm not sure, really. But he *has* been acting kind of strange lately."

"My parents act strange *a lot*," Jude teased.

"No, but I mean it's like I can't do anything right when I'm around him. Or, let's say, if I ask him for a ride somewhere, you'd think I was hitting him up for a hundred dollars. He never acted like that before."

"Yeah, he'd take us everywhere. Remember how on Saturdays we'd go down to one of his bridge sites and he'd let us ride in the crane?"

"I used to love that. He always said, 'I'm gonna show you girls the City of Bridges the way nobody ever sees it!'"

"How come we weren't scared, up that high?" Jude wondered.

"Beats me. Shelley was always scared, though. She quit coming with us after a few times, remember?"

"We were too little to know any better. I'd be scared to death to go up that high now, except maybe in an elevator!"

Hallie fiddled with her watchband. "Hey, I better get going! Mom thinks I'm asking you about home-work. She'll have a fit if I don't set the table on time."

"Well, good luck. Look at it this way. Maybe your dad never saw you guys. Your mom won't say any-thing, will she?"

"Who knows? Keep your fingers crossed. See you tomorrow, Jude."

Once inside her house, Hallie stopped short of the kitchen, overhearing her mother's voice in staccato bits and phrases.

"Not even *looking* for jobs anymore." Pause. "I'm at work most of the day. As far as I can tell . . . Spends his time down in the garage." Pause. "Welding." Pause. "I don't know, Kay. . . . Wouldn't call it sculpture. . . . Looks like junk to me." Hallie tried not to breathe so she could hear each word. "Just can't seem to give it up, since he's not building bridges." Pause. "I know, I know . . . but it's all he seems to care about."

Too late for the table now. Unnoticed, Hallie slipped

upstairs before her mother hung up the phone. She tried to start her homework, but those words pricked her like a pin. *It's all he seems to care about.* When had she heard those words before? The night her father first lost his job. . . .

"Jim! Keep your voice down. The girls!"

Hallie tiptoed out into the upstairs hallway. Shelley was already perched halfway down the steps, craning her neck between the twisted iron bars of the railing. Disapproving, she gave Hallie a stern one-word-and-I'll-kill-you look. Hallie could not keep quiet. "What's going on down there?" she asked. Shelley put her finger to her lips.

"Those SOB's. I'd like to . . ." The sound of a cupboard opening, slamming. "Fattening their own pockets. . . . It's us little guys . . ." *Clink, clink, clink.* Running water.

"Even the mills are closing, Jim. Times are tough everywhere right now."

"Well, you can't tell me the city of Pittsburgh just ran out of money. For God's sake, Louise. In one day— to lay off a hundred or more men?"

"It's not the end of the world. You'll find something else."

Hallie elbowed Shelley. "Did Daddy lose his job?" No answer. "Why did Daddy lose his job?"

Shelley shrugged.

"A good three years' worth of work . . . Bridge is three-quarters finished. . . ." The sound of a chair knocked over.

"I think you've had enough."

"Don't tell me—"

"Please, Jim."

Silence.

"You don't understand. It's all I care about." Her father's voice, breaking. "I just want to be up there in the iron. . . ."

Orphaned by her parents' argument, Hallie ran downstairs and pounded out "Chopsticks" on the living room piano, louder than they could ignore—anything to drown the sound, make them stop.

"Not now, honey," her mother called, straining to speak kindly. She heard her father swear, followed by the smack of the door to the basement, a single sharp blow to the house. Hallie could have counted each of her father's fourteen angry footsteps as he stormed downstairs, had she tried.

She didn't dare enter the kitchen. She turned back up the stairs. And away. Shelley had disappeared behind her bedroom door. There was no sign that said DO NOT ENTER, but Hallie felt prohibited. She knocked anyway. Nothing. "I know you're in there, Shelley."

Testing the knob, she found the door locked. She pressed an ear against the hard plane of wood, thought she heard Shelley crying. In that moment, Hallie hated her sister. Not just for shutting her out. They had each overheard the same words, the same argument. But while the knowledge hurt Shelley, Hallie did not know enough to cry.

3

Hallie's mother breathed not a word about their escapade in the car—until dessert. "Have you thought about going down to Sears, Jim, and putting in an application?" she asked finally.

"No-I-have-not-thought-about-going-down-to-Sears-and-putting-in-an-application!" her father mimicked.

For one entire minute, nobody spoke. Not a syllable. Not a sigh. Her father twisted his wedding ring from his finger, set it on top of the saltshaker, twirled it around and around. It was the only sound, that twirling. *Whirrlll, whirrlll, whirrlll,* as persistent as the ticking of a clock. It was more than a nervous habit with him, more than an idle game. "Jim, I . . ." As if a button had been pressed or a key wound, Hallie stood, abandoning her ice cream, and began mechanically clearing away the dishes.

Then both her parents were speaking at once. "I never said—" "Don't think I don't know—" "You can't—" Hallie imagined countless other dinner-table conversations taking place that same evening, in countless other households. "How was school today, honey? Pass the pepper. Do you have a lot of homework? The peas, please." She purposefully rattled the silverware to let them know she was alive. And in the same room.

Hallie reached across her father's empty plate for the teapot. "I said, leave the tea, damn it!" her father yelled. As if disconnected from her own body, Hallie watched the china pot fall from her hand. Shatter. Broken shards swam in a small pond of tea gone cold. Shirtfront dripping, her father stood fiercely and shook his hands like someone coming in after a hard rain.

Without a word, he yanked the edge of his place mat, fast—the way a magician whisks a tablecloth from under dishes in one swoop. Plates clattered against the table in a kind of drumroll. Her mother gasped and Hallie ran from the room.

Fled upstairs. Wrapped herself in a patched-up old quilt that smelled of her grandmother's cedar chest, closing out the shouts in a cocoon, dark and safe. She imagined herself a bug, a slug, a thick wet gooey caterpillar inside its chrysalis, waiting for wings on which to escape.

She lay there for a time with her eyes squeezed tight, not sure if she slept. The scene, in slow motion, replayed itself. *I didn't hear him say not to take away his stupid tea. Why is he so mad?*

When she crawled from her quilt-cocoon hours later, she was still in yesterday's clothes. Someone had turned off the light without waking her. Already, gray morning light edged its way in the cracks around the blinds. She sat in the semidarkness, opened the blinds, and stared at the rain on the windowpane, trying to trace the path of a single drop to its destination, but one always poured into another and she lost track.

Only the hypnotic sounds of the rain disturbed the quiet: *thrummm* against the window, *plink plink* when it hit a pipe. For the first time, Hallie heard the rain. Really heard. As if it were music, she separated the strings from the horns, the reeds from the percussion.

Maybe it was the rain that hatched a particular memory in her mind just then. A memory of something so familiar. Lines from a poem—a poem her mother had often recited at bedtime.

Let the rain kiss you.
Let the rain beat upon your head with silver liquid drops.
Let the rain sing you a lullaby.

The lines reminded her again of her homework. The poem about spring. She still hadn't started it! What could she possibly say about spring? Everything had been said before. . . .

Sourly, Hallie gazed at the sky, heavy and bloated, the color of old snow. *Can't say that,* she thought. *Spring poems are supposed to be cheerful.*

The rain let up but hung from every branch, leaf, blade of grass, dripped from the eaves of the roof, gushed still from the gutters.

Hallie stared at her sheet of paper, at her name and homeroom number in the corner. The floor creaked. When she was little and heard noises in the night, her dad had always told her, "Go back to bed, sweetie. It's just the house settling." She never understood those words, never imagined a house as a place that shifted or changed. Or became different. . . .

Footsteps. Was it already time for her mother to be up? Pipes clanged, followed by the gurgle of water. She hurriedly scribbled some lines about rain on her paper. Something. Anything. *So I flunk English! Who cares?*

Hallie crawled into bed and pulled the covers up to her chin, feigning sleep. She couldn't face conversation yet. Only the familiar smell of her pillow comforted her this morning.

She heard the rustle of a slip as her mother padded up the hall. The door opened. Eyes shut, Hallie sensed her mother leaning over her. *I hope she can't hear my heart pounding.* Hallie willed herself not to move her eyeballs beneath their lids. *What's taking her so long?* She hardly dared exhale.

The closet door slid open on its rollers. The squeak of hangers against the metal rod. Her mother sighing, searching for a skirt for work from her half of the closet. Then, nothing but the swish of silky-sounding stockings, and her mother was gone.

I I I I I I I I

4

Hallie and her father passed in the hall that morning like two hands of a clock headed in the same direction but not touching. *He must still be in a bad mood,* Hallie thought. When he did speak to her downstairs, he tightened his lips nervously and asked, "Did you get your allowance this week?" *He knows I got it, but doesn't know what else to say.* "Here. Here's a five. For new clothes or something."

"Dad, you don't have to—"

"Just keep it, Hallie. I'll win it back from you in Scrabble someday."

"Dad, we haven't played Scrabble since Shelley left!"

"Consider it an advance on grass cutting, then," he said, twisting the doorknob back and forth.

"Thanks, Dad." She squeezed out the words unenthusiastically, tossing the money into the gaping mouth of her backpack. "I don't want to miss the bus. Bye."

Dreading English class, Hallie dragged herself into school on Tuesday. She tried to tuck the memory of her father's rage into the back corner of her mind, but the image loomed there like a shadow created by candlelight.

By Friday, the class had not heard a word about their poems. "D day," Jude whispered.

"Literally," Hallie joked back. She crossed her fingers on both hands and sat on them, holding out for a C.

Miss Sands, her seventh-grade English teacher, had the biggest eyes Hallie had ever seen, and they always appeared to hurt. Today was no exception. "Class . . ." Her eyes beseeched them. *Here it comes, the speech.* "I have to say that, on the whole, I am rather disappointed with the poems you handed in."

What did she expect with a topic like spring?

"I purposely assigned this topic to stretch you, to make you think, to take an old, tired subject and make it fresh."

Who is she kidding?

"I read e. e. cummings, with his words like *mud-luscious* and *puddle-wonderful* to give you a sense of what can be done if you use your imaginations. I have chosen a few poems that I think are exceptional, which I'll read to you. I want everyone to listen to the language, to think about what makes these poems different. Then I want you others to rethink your own poems over the weekend."

Groans and murmurs all around. *Not again! I couldn't think of an idea the first time.*

"I'll start with a haiku by David Mooney." *David Mooney! He wouldn't know haiku from karate.*

Next, Christina Wheat.

So intent was Hallie on biting the skin around her nails that all she heard was "new green willows" and "maple seeds hung like berries." *Maybe I could go up to Miss Sands after class,* she schemed silently. *Talk to her. Tell her, not what really happened, but maybe . . .*

". . . most creative approach is Henrietta O'Shea's poem."

Hallie hardly recognized the name. *Me! She means me!* She had reminded Miss Sands to call her Hallie at least a hundred times, but the woman insisted on addressing students by their full names as printed on her class roster. *She must have made a mistake. My poem? Don't read it, Miss Sands. Please do not read it in front of the whole class.*

"This is an example of concrete poetry."

It is?

"We haven't studied this yet, class, but in concrete poetry, the poem actually takes on the shape of its subject. In this case, a raindrop. Or a teardrop. Henrietta has given us a fine example."

She has? I mean, I have?

"I'll write it on the board to demonstrate."

No, please don't! Hallie wanted to shout.

Rain
drops
like tears on
the black branches
of the wet limbs
of the trees
of April

Kevin, a classmate Hallie knew only by the back of his collar, turned around and said, "Hey, Hallie. That's really neat how you did that."

"Thanks," she mumbled, feeling like a hypocrite, not wanting anyone to know that her poem was just an accident.

Concealing a note written on her palm, Jude surreptitiously slid her hand under the desk, then flashed it at Hallie. Hallie leaned into the aisle, pretending to pick up a pencil she had dropped. I THINK HE LIKES YOU!

YOU'RE CRAZY! HE HASN'T SAID TWO WORDS TO ME ALL YEAR! Hallie scrawled in her notebook, then showed Jude when Miss Sands wasn't looking.

"I will post these poems on the bulletin board, class, so that everyone may take a closer look. I want the rest of you to think about these, but when you sit down to write, try to find your own words, your own language, your own form and shape."

"I know how to find form and shape," said Frank Pearl, class clown, describing curves with his hands for the benefit of those in the back rows.

A snicker spread through the room. Kevin turned around again and rolled his eyes. *All because of a poem that I didn't even know was concrete!*

"Hallie, wait up." She was making her getaway from St. Scholastica when the out-of-breath voice stopped her.

"I just wanted to tell you . . . I saw your poem. In Miss Sands's room, I mean. I'm Crane. Henderson. My brother knows your sister and everything. I mean, that's how I knew who you were. After Miss Sands told me, I ran all the way because I thought you'd be catching the early bus. I liked it. . . . The poem, I mean."

Hallie couldn't speak. Couldn't think. Call it shy, or just plain dumbfounded. Here was Crane Henderson from the high school, the familiar freshman everybody called "Monk," running down the hall to catch up with her. Crane Henderson, who took pictures for the school newspaper, who knew everyone in the middle school and high school and was even friendly with the teachers. That Crane.

"Say something," he said finally. He had a way of nodding his head when he talked, so that his straight black hair fell in his eyes.

"Thanks, I guess."

"What do you mean, *you guess*?"

Hallie soon found herself confessing. "I mean, I didn't even write the poem. Well, I wrote it, but I didn't mean to. It was sort of an accident. I couldn't think of anything else to write. I just sort of did it fast, but the shape of the raindrop and everything, that had nothing to do with me." She could tell her words were scarcely making sense.

Just thinking about it later made her blush. Crane Henderson, of all people. A stranger! If only he hadn't asked if he could walk with her. Then taken the bus with her. *It wasn't even his bus!*

And what was it he had said? "It does have to do with you." What did he mean by that?

She went over and over it in her mind, wondering if he could be right, wondering if there *was* something inside of her that made her write the poem that way, something that even she did not understand. A chill ran from the base of her neck up the back of her skull.

Wondering if they would cross paths again . . . somehow.

5

No amount of hoping helped Hallie run into Crane the following week. Wanting something to happen was no longer as simple as wishing it on a birthday candle or blowing away a stray eyelash.

Nose pressed to the window, she sat by herself in the back of the bus, wishing Jude hadn't stayed for band practice. "Hey, scootch over. You think you own this seat or something?" There he was, grinning at her, his dark eyes teasing beneath his shock of thick hair.

"Crane, hi!" She moved her backpack from the seat beside her. "Sorry, I didn't know this seat had your name on it," she teased back.

"You didn't? Well, that's because it's way down here." He flopped onto the floor of the bus, then stretched out flat on his back like a mechanic underneath a car.

"Crane! You're crazy. Get up."

"Not until you look. I can tell you don't believe me."

"I don't *believe* you're lying on the floor of this bus. It's filthy dirty down there. You probably have gum stuck in your hair this very second."

"I'm not moving till you look."

Hallie hung her head upside down to look under the seat.

"See?" He pointed to the crooked letters that spelled MONK.

"Okay, okay, I believe you."

Once he was seated, she said, "You just wrote that right now. I should report you to the bus driver for writing graffiti. Defacing public property!"

"I'm at your mercy," Crane pleaded, with folded hands. "Let this be our secret," he whispered. "Besides, it'll wash off, I swear."

"You're nuts, you know that?"

"So I've been told."

"Hey, Monk!" a kid in the back row called to him. "What were you looking for down there, huh?"

"Wouldn't you like to know." Crane laughed, but he turned to Hallie and said, "Don't mind him."

"Why do they call you Monk anyway?" Hallie asked, curiosity overcoming her.

"Oh, that. It's a long story."

"This ought to be good."

"It's dumb, really."

"Look, it can't be much worse than Henrietta."

"I thought I heard Miss Sands call you that. How'd you get Hallie, then?"

"Wouldn't you if your name was Henrietta?"

"Well, yeah, but . . ."

"See, I came home crying one day in elementary school because the kids were teasing me. David

Mooney made up a saying, like a little chant, that he got all the kids to say. 'Hen-ri-et-ta is a bed wet-ter.'"

Crane groaned. "Oh no."

"Oh yes. My mother tried to convince me that Henrietta's a great name. 'It's your grandmother's name,' she always said. She told me I should be proud and everything like that. But the next day I marched into school and told the teacher my name was Hallie. Like Hayley Mills in that movie *The Trouble with Angels,* only I was pronouncing it wrong." *Why am I telling him this stupid story?*

"Don't feel bad. My grandmother called me her little Crane-berry. Still does. Get it, like *cran*berry?" They both laughed. The bus was chugging up the hill now, making the turn toward her street.

"Do you take this bus only sometimes?" she blurted out, changing the subject.

"Only when I see girls with green eyes and green backpacks get on."

Hallie felt her face grow hot.

"No, seriously," he said. "I get off at Shramm's Farm, just down Thompson Run Road from here."

Her heart sank. She should have guessed. Darlene Shramm was in the same grade as Crane. "You know Darlene Shramm?"

"Of course. That's how I got a job there and everything."

"Job?" Hallie knew she sounded incredulous.

"Sure, you know those things where you work a certain number of hours and they pay you money for it?"

"What do you do there?"

"Oh, I help out a few days a week, mostly with their animals. It beats delivering papers. Keeps me off the streets, my mom says."

"I didn't know they had a lot of animals. Oops, this is it. My stop," Hallie said, climbing over Crane's legs. "Hey, you still didn't tell me about your nickname."

"Well, another time. Can I call you?" Crane asked.

"Sure . . ." She shrugged, not knowing what to say. "I guess."

"What do you mean, you guess?" Crane asked for the second time, calling out the bus window as she walked down the street.

Hallie laughed, barely hearing him above the grinding of gears as the bus pulled away.

She walked home slowly, thinking he never really would, thinking she hadn't given him her phone number, wondering why he thought he had to ask.

The house was dead quiet. No sounds of ringing metal from the garage. Hallie sighed. Her father was gone. . . . Without stopping for a snack, she went straight to her room. She was glad to have the house to herself. Room to think her own thoughts.

Hallie had seen the sign for Shramm's Farm/Dairy hundreds of times but never paid much attention. Now it took on new meaning. Darlene Shramm was suddenly elevated to celebrity status.

Hallie longed to tell someone, anyone, about her encounter with Crane. *But not Jude*, she warned herself. *Then everybody at school will find out and make a big deal over it. Pretty soon the whole seventh grade will think I have a crush on him or something when I've talked to him two times.*

"Crane." She tested the word aloud, as if her lips had never formed the sound before. *What an unusual name. And to think Jude and I were just talking about riding in the crane,* Hallie remembered with secret delight.

If only Shelley hadn't gone away . . .

Whenever Hallie missed her sister, she pulled out the note Shelley had written the morning she left for college, and read it again, smiling.

> Dear Hallie,
>   Time has slipped through my fingers and crept up on me. Now I must heed its call and carry with me my most precious possessions, inside my heart. I leave a most important part of me behind with you. . . . Please take good care of it.
>   The miles will separate us now, but I promise you they will never change things, for we are too much a part of each other. I love you so, so much, Hallie, and will think of you always.
>   Love, Shelley

Today it made her cry.

Hallie tiptoed into her sister's room, as if being surrounded by Shelley's things might bring her back. The room was tidy and smelled faintly of furniture polish. She felt curiously hollow sitting there in the rocker her father had painted for them, the rocker they had shared until a few years ago, when Shelley pleaded for her own room. She remembered crying then, too.

Shelley seemed so far away now. Although she called weekly on Sunday nights, their mother stayed on the other extension, so Hallie couldn't really talk. *Not about Crane. Or Dad.*

Trying to cheer herself, Hallie thought, *She'll be home soon for spring break. Only a week to go. . . .*

Sounds of clanging metal disturbed the quiet. Her father must have returned. Hallie wished he would show her whatever it was he was working on down there. Or tell her about it. They'd hardly spoken since that night. The night she broke the teapot. Living with him was like looking at someone through the wrong end of binoculars. He was right there, close, but seemed very far away.

Hallie scanned her sister's shelves. A miniature china tea set, Larry Lion, her porcelain horse collection . . . *I used to love to touch them, even though I wasn't allowed,* Hallie remembered.

"You'll break them. You have your own," Shelley used to say. But Hallie's were cats. Siamese, calico, you name it. Every birthday, her mother had given her a small statue of a cat. She didn't even like cats.

She lifted the mustang, turning it in her hands. Shelley's favorite. The one she called Pie, after the horse in *National Velvet*. Frozen in motion, he was forever running in the wind, his mane blown back. Hurricane would be a better name, she'd always thought. One leg was broken, from the time Hallie, in a fit of temper, threw her shoe at her sister's shelf.

She wondered why Shelley hadn't taken the collection with her. . . .

The tuna fish casserole! She'd forgotten it. Hallie jumped up with a start the second she remembered, ran downstairs, flicked on the oven. Now dinner would be late. And *both* Mom and Dad would be angry.

6

The phone rang, startling their dinnertime silence like a dropped knife. "Hallie? Yes, just a minute. She's right here," her mother answered, sounding overly polite. "For you, Hallie. It's a boy."

"Mo-om!" Hallie rolled her eyes exasperatedly. "I'll get it upstairs."

"Give me that phone," she heard her father say, and took the steps two at a time. She picked up the receiver. "Don't you kids know any better than to call in the middle of a meal?"

"Dad! I got it!" Hallie said urgently. "You can hang up now. . . . Hello?"

"Hello, Hallie? It's me, Crane. I'm sorry. I didn't know you'd be eating."

"No, it's okay."

"Really? I hope I didn't . . ."

"Honest. We don't usually eat this late. It was my fault." A feeble attempt at an apology. Her heart was thumping. *From running up the steps? Or because it's Crane?*

"I can't really talk. I just wanted to ask you, I

mean . . ." His voice lowered to merely a whisper.

"Crane, where are you?"

"I'm at home."

Hallie knew Crane had several brothers and sisters, but she heard no noise in the background.

"Listen, I gotta go, but I was just wondering if there's any way, I mean . . . you're probably busy or something. I should have asked you before, but I have to work tomorrow and I was thinking maybe we could do something when I get off, you know, like . . . together, if you want to."

"Um, well . . ."

"Look, it's okay if you don't want to. No big deal or anything. I thought we could take a walk or something."

"Yeah, sure," Hallie said. "What time do you think you'll be done?"

"How about—is it okay if I just come over, maybe around eleven?"

"I'll be here."

"Great. Sorry I can't talk. I'll see you tomorrow then, Hallie. Thanks and everything. Okay, bye."

Why is he acting so mysterious? Hallie wondered, but before she thought to ask, he'd hung up. "Bye, Crane," she whispered to the dial tone.

The instant she put the phone down, it rang again and her heart skipped a beat. "Crane?"

"Hallie? It's me, Jude. Who'dya think it was?"

"Oh, hi, Jude. Nobody." She was hoping Jude hadn't caught the name.

"Can you go?"

"Go?" Hallie asked.

"To the movies. You didn't forget, did you? Hey, did you say Crane? You mean Crane Henderson?"

Oh no, Jude did hear. "No, I didn't really forget. I just haven't had a chance to ask yet."

"Well, go ask. I'll hang on."

"You haven't even finished your dinner," her mother said. Predictable.

"That's all I can eat, Mom. I'm not hungry anymore. I can get popcorn at the movies and I'll do the dishes when I get home, I promise." All in one breath.

Jude said, "Meet us at the manhole in ten minutes," when Hallie agreed to go. She splashed water on her face and ran a brush through her wavy brown hair, willing it straight. No use. Shelley had the thick, straight hair. Her sister always consoled her with, "You have those shiny red highlights," which Hallie failed to see. Grabbing a sweater, she called out, "Bye!" from the safe distance of the hallway. Being quizzed about her phone call was bad enough. She'd rather it came from Jude than her mother.

Once, in second grade, she and Jude had gone to great trouble to measure and find the exact midpoint between the front doors of their two houses—the manhole. Over the years, it doubled as pitcher's mound, imaginary snake pit, and now, favorite meeting place.

The Jacobses' car was waiting.

"Hi, Mr. Jacobs," Hallie said, climbing into the backseat.

"How's my other daughter?" he asked.

"I'm doing okay."

"Jude tells me you're going out for the lead in the school play."

"Jude! I am not," Hallie protested. "It's Charlie Brown!"

"He knows. That's why he's teasing you. Almost all the roles are boys anyway," Jude said.

"Besides, Mr. Jacobs, I can't sing."

"How about Schroeder? All he does is play Beethoven. You play piano, Hallie. Just because you're girls . . . In fact, we've encouraged Jude to try out for Pigpen. Right, Jude?"

"Very funny, Dad." Jude rolled her eyes at Hallie. "Let *me* talk to my friend now, okay?"

"Okay, okay, I forgot. I'm just the driver." Mr. Jacobs smiled at Hallie in the rearview mirror.

Jude yanked Hallie's sleeve, pulling her closer. "I don't ride the bus with you for one lousy week and look what happens—you go getting yourself a boyfriend!"

"He's not my *boy*friend, Jude."

"Oh, I get it. You always pick up the phone and ask if it's someone who's *not* your boyfriend."

"Jude, I just met him. I only talked to him a few times. Honest." Hallie told her about Crane running up and complimenting her on the poem. At first, telling Jude was a relief. Afterward, Hallie felt awkward, as if she'd given away a secret.

Jude kept saying, "I can't believe it—Crane Henderson. Let me get this straight. First he chases you down the hall. Then takes your bus. *Then* calls you on the phone that same night. . . ."

"Jude, it's not like . . ."

"My own best friend! He's in ninth grade, Hallie. High school."

"I know what grade he's in," Hallie said. She tried to distract Jude by asking about the movie.

"Well, when are you going out?"

"We're not going out, Jude." It wasn't exactly a lie. *We're just going for a walk.*

Hallie welcomed the dark of the theater, where she could often forget herself. But during all the slow parts, her mind kept drifting back to Crane and their walk the next day. *It's no big deal, right?* she asked herself. She had practically confided in Jude. But not quite.

She twisted the button of her sweater one too many times. It dropped into her hand. What would it be like? With Crane? Tomorrow?

7

What if he doesn't know which house it is? Did I forget to tell him? Hallie paced from bed to window in Shelley's room, ears alert to each and every sound. A squeaky bicycle in the drive? A possible knock at the door? Just a squirrel barking in the oak tree out front. The scrape of her father's chair against the wall downstairs.

It wasn't at all as she imagined. He arrived without a sound. Didn't come up the walk. Or knock. Stood under her father's straggly plum tree, inspecting the tips of its branches for new buds, peeling back the craggy bark.

"Crane! Hi!"

"Hallie! I was just . . . What kind of tree is this anyway?"

As she told him, they took the path that led from Hallie's dead-end street through the woods and down to the abandoned railroad tracks. Just walking next to Crane, Hallie felt nervous, jittery with anticipation.

"If you follow these tracks far enough, there's a steep hill you can climb that takes you right up to the back of Shramm's," he was saying.

"Is that how you came, then? You walked all that way?"

"Sure. Only a couple of miles, really. I like to walk. Sometimes on Saturdays I ride my bike to work, though."

"I just can't believe about the Shramms. I knew they had a little store, but I didn't think there were any farms left around here."

"This whole area used to be farms, Mr. Shramm says. Nothing but cows and muddy roads. Now he's got the last ten acres that haven't been bought up for houses."

"What kind of stuff did you say you do, Crane?"

"Well, on Saturdays, like today, I get there real early and feed and water the animals. I usually play with the dogs a while before Mr. Shramm tells me what he needs me to do. I talk to the sheep and the goat while I give them fresh hay. You know, stuff like that. Then, of course, there're the stalls. Shoveling them out takes a while. Oh, by the way, sorry if I smell like a barn. Mom always says I do on Saturdays."

To Hallie, Crane smelled clean, like a just-washed apple. "Um . . . Doesn't anybody else help you?" she asked.

"Oh, Mr. Shramm does the work, really. He's got some kids who are older. They used to do a lot, but they're mostly gone now. So he has me, and I just kind of fit in where I can."

"Sounds like you don't mind it, though."

"I don't. I mean, it can get pretty crazy around our house with all my brothers and sisters, you know. There're still five of us at home."

"I guess you kind of . . . need a break from that."

"Yeah, and what I like is, if I get to work early, before everybody wakes up, it's real quiet there. If I'm lucky, the dogs will kick up a deer and I'll just barely catch a flash of white through the trees. I know there's a real pretty doe that lives by the creek, because sometimes I get to watch her drinking. Or we'll stand there, absolutely still, looking at each other—like the way my one little brother always makes me have a stare-down contest with him."

"A what?"

"I'll show you." Crane led Hallie by the arm and sat her down on a railroad tie. He sat right across from her.

"Now, elbows on your knees. Hold your head in your hands and stare at me. I stare back at you, and then we see who can go the longest without blinking."

Hallie tried, but as soon as she looked directly into those buck eyes of his, she became acutely aware of her crooked nose, the moon-shaped dent in her left cheek from a childhood fall. She laughed, embarrassed. "How can you do it? I keep cracking up."

"Practice. Believe me, I get lots of practice."

"Then who wins, you or the deer?"

"She does. Always. So I decided—maybe deer don't blink. Think about it. Did you ever see one blink?"

"Oh, Crane! I have no idea." Hallie laughed.

They followed the tracks a long way, balancing like tightrope walkers on the rails or jumping from one tie to the next. Every so often, Crane would lean down to study something on the ground.

"Looking for a lucky stone?" Hallie asked him.

"Lucky stone?"

"Yes. You know, one with a hole that goes all the way through the middle. A real lucky stone is hard to find."

"Ever find one?"

"Me? Only once, at the ocean."

"Then you're lucky." He grinned.

Hallie soon saw that Crane was a collector of things, as she was. He picked up a white-tipped blue-jay feather, a mud-caked marble, a comic from a Bazooka bubble-gum wrapper. Laughing, he read aloud the fortune: "What you think won't happen won't."

"What's that supposed to mean?" she asked.

"Who knows? You have to believe in something for it to happen, I guess. These things are always crazy-sounding." She saw him tuck the fortune in the tiny watch pocket of his jeans.

He spied the head of a purple crocus poking up under the leaves and pointed to it. He stood still, weight on one leg. Imitated a whippoorwill's call.

"Listen! It's answering back. It must think you're another bird!" Hallie laughed delightedly.

While Crane noticed everything around them, Hallie noticed him. The ripped knee of his jeans, his arm brushing against hers while they walked. At first she crammed both hands inside the pouch of her sweatshirt. Then she tried letting them dangle at her sides.

All of a sudden, Crane said, "Shhh!"

"I wasn't talking."

"Shhh!" He leaned over close and whispered into her hair, then covered her mouth briefly. His hand was warm, thick and leathery like her dad's hands. She smiled, remembering how her father used to stick pins in his calluses, then clutch his wrist, pretending to be in pain until she and Shelley came to the rescue with kisses.

"A woodpecker. Listen." Hallie's eyes followed Crane's, scanning the tops of trees at the edge of the woods, and spotted the largest redheaded woodpecker she'd ever seen.

"A pileated!" Crane whispered excitedly. "I wish we had binoculars. You don't get to see them much." It darted inside the hollow of a dead tree.

"Look!" She pointed. "It's spring-cleaning." The woodpecker was gathering leaves in its beak, tossing them out of the hole.

"Sure is!" The woodpecker ducked back inside the tree.

"Hey, look, up higher. It went to the top floor!"

"Hear that sound it's making, *t-t-t-t-t*? Did you know it's not just drilling for grubs, but that's how they communicate, too, like if they want to attract attention?" He turned to her, flicking the hair from his eyes.

The woods was suddenly quiet.

Hallie wanted not to move. Instead, she said, "We better head back, don't you think? I mean, we've walked a long way." She headed along the path in the other direction.

"Are you writing any more poems, Hallie?"

"Um . . . not really. No. Not since the one for Miss Sands."

"Hey, maybe you could get one in the school newspaper."

"I don't think so. . . ." Hallie laughed. "Shelley's the writer in our family."

"Miss Sands says you're good."

Hallie wanted to change the subject. "How come you still go down to the middle school to talk to her? Do you know her or something?"

"Only from seventh-grade English, same as you. I just like her, I guess."

"But, I mean, what do you talk about?"

"About books, mostly—I don't know. See, my parents were always on my case because I didn't read. The only thing you could get me to pick up was *National Geographic*, and that was mainly for the pictures. Then, in seventh grade, Miss Sands gave me *The Call of the Wild*. Jack London. Read it yet?"

Hallie shook her head no but thought then of going to the library to check it out.

"It's this incredible adventure story. Takes place in Alaska where the guy's dog, Buck, saves his life and everything. More than once. It's based on a true story. And Miss Sands knows stuff about Jack London. How he slept only four hours a night and wrote all the rest of the time. He even rigged up an alarm clock that dropped a weight on his head just to make sure he'd wake up!" Crane gestured enthusiastically with his hands.

Hallie stopped walking. Imitating Crane, she waved her arms wildly, exaggerating his gestures.

Crane laughed. "I guess I get carried away, huh?"

"No, it's perfectly normal to talk with your hands," Hallie teased him, "like this."

"Okay, that does it." Crane chased Hallie. She ran down the path as fast as she could, trying not to trip on the tentacles of thick roots underfoot. Finally she collapsed on the ground, out of breath. Crane fell beside her.

"Okay, okay, I give up. Truce," Hallie panted.

"You're the one who started it."

"Who, me?"

"Asking about Miss Sands. You're lucky you have her this year. I wish she'd move up to the high school, but she says she'll never leave seventh grade. She says that's where a teacher can really make a difference."

"Yeah, but I have Miss Cabussi, too, don't forget."

"Science, right? Do they still call her . . . ?"

"The Caboose!" they said at the same time.

"You better watch out for her. She's an air force sergeant, and she knows karate *and* judo."

"Great. She has it in for me, too." Hallie stood, brushing off the seat of her pants, and started walking again.

"How come?" Crane asked, catching up with her.

"Well, she wanted us to turn in a pro-spec-tus"—Hallie enunciated each syllable—"about our science projects. I still don't have an idea, and we were supposed to work on it over a monthlong period."

"When's it due?"

"Friday morning. They have to be in before Easter weekend."

"Whoa! That soon. Well, you might not like this idea, but I've done a project with mice. You build a maze and put cheese, like a reward, at the end. Then you watch the mice try to get through the maze every day, and you see if they get any better at it, like maybe they learned something."

"Hey, that sounds neat. Do you think I'd have time, with just a week left?"

"If you got the mice right away, that's all you'd really need. I mean, you could use my cage and everything. You'd have to build a new maze, but I think I still have a drawing of the one I used, if you want that."

"You mean it, really? That'd be great, Crane. Saved . . . from the wrath of the Caboose."

They were nearing the end of the path now. Hallie could see the roof of her house through the new green on the trees. Crane touched the back of her arm and said, "Hallie, about last night, when I couldn't talk . . ."

"It's okay, Crane. You don't have to explain."

"No, I want to. See, my parents have this idea. With eight kids and everything, they think it's good to have a quiet time. I mean, not just to yourself, but a family thing, where you don't talk. It gives everybody a break for a little while."

"You mean not say anything, not even a word?"

"Right."

"For how long?"

"Couple of hours. Every night between seven and nine, we're not supposed to talk. I know it sounds kind of crazy, but anyway, that's why I had to whisper. Now you know how I got called Monk. This guy Jeff started it when he found out last year, and it kind of stuck."

Crane looked over at Hallie. Since he got no answer, he asked, "What are you thinking?"

"Nothing. Except that I better get going." She had been thinking that she liked the name Crane better. Monk seemed like an inside joke that did not include her. Monk was the Crane Henderson in ninth grade, the Crane with the high school friends, the Crane that Hallie knew nothing about.

They said good-bye awkwardly. As Hallie turned to go, Crane stretched his hand in the air, turned it into a wave. She could feel him watching her leave. It was later that she caught herself wondering: had he been reaching toward her? Maybe to hold her hand? Or to touch her hair before disappearing back into the woods, as softly as he had come.

8

"Mom, do you think we could go to the pet store and get some mice?"

"Mice?"

"Not for pets. For my Science Fair project. Crane built this really neat maze and he said I could use his plans to build one, and it shows you all about if mice can learn."

"Honey, that's more for biology class, isn't it? Crane's in high school. Why can't you just make something simple, like a volcano?"

"Mom, do you know how many volcanoes there will be at the Science Fair?"

"Well, ask your father. It's up to him if he wants to get involved with maze building."

Hallie tentatively poked her head around the unfinished doorjamb in the den, where her father was watching television.

"Dad, can I get some mice, you know, for my Science Fair project? Crane says—"

"Talk to your mother," he interrupted.

"She says it's up to you because—"

"Hallie, can't you see I'm trying to watch?"

"I know, Dad. Look, I can get the mice. All I want to know is, will you help me build the maze part?"

No answer. Hallie wondered if her father had heard her. She eased herself down next to him on the couch.

"Can't this wait, Hallie?" he asked, his eyes never leaving the television.

"But I have to turn it in next week."

Silence. Finally: "And you're telling me now?" He glanced sideways at her, then back to the movie.

Hallie looked away, stared at the screen. It was an old movie in black and white, and the people talked hurriedly.

"Dad, I mean . . . I need you. . . ."

"Okay, okay. I'll help. Later. Now just watch."

Hallie watched, feeling mildly triumphant. A man was crawling belly-down through a pine forest.

"What's he doing?"

"He's spying on a bridge."

"A bridge?" *I should have known,* she thought, glancing over at him, suddenly wishing herself five again. Young enough to curl up in his lap. "What is this movie anyway?"

"For Whom the Bell Tolls."

"Who's that?"

"Gary Cooper—that's him there—is an American living in Spain, and there's a civil war going on. He's in with a band of guerrillas hiding out in the mountains. They're sending him to blow up a strategic bridge."

"Why is he sketching?"

"He's studying the bridge from all angles. Then he

makes sketches so he can plan it out. He has only a split second to detonate the bridge at the exact right moment. Now . . ." He held up his hand to silence her.

Hallie sat hugging her knees on the couch, trying not to ask any more questions. But during the final scene, she couldn't help herself. "Tell me what happens," she blurted, covering her eyes, then peeking through her fingers. The bridge exploded in the background. An enemy officer approached on horseback. "Oh no. He has a broken leg. He'll never get away now!" She turned her head so as not to see. When she looked again, Gary Cooper lay facedown in the snow. "What happened?"

"He got shot." Her father stood up and turned off the television.

"That's the end? I can't believe it. After all that? What's the whole point, then, if he died anyway?"

"The point is the bridge, Hallie. Whether he lived or died is insignificant. The bridge is what unified the peasants; it wasn't him. The bridge gave them a purpose, don't you see?"

"But it was all for nothing. I mean, they didn't even win their freedom."

"It wasn't all for nothing, Hallie."

She sensed it was time to change the subject. "So you'll help me with the science project?"

He walked over to the bookshelves, cleared his throat. "I said I would," he answered, his back toward her. He picked up his transistor radio, stretched the antenna to its full length, tuned in the ball game, and turned up the volume.

9

"Why didn't you wait for me, Dad?"

When Hallie arrived home from church on Sunday, her father was already sawing away, cutting out rectangular pieces of wood.

"I thought you had to get going on this."

"I do, but I wanted to show you the design for the maze first. The one Crane's giving me."

"This isn't for a maze."

"Then what's it for?"

"There's not enough time to fool with mice, Hallie. We'll build a motor. I know a really simple one. Saw it in *Life* magazine years ago. All we'll need are—"

"Pencil and a paper clip," Hallie said knowingly.

"Right."

"But, Dad, that's just what you told Shelley. It *does* take long, and she ended up having to use a battery anyway! I really want to do something different, like the mice."

"You know how your mother feels about animals in the house."

"You said we could yesterday!"

"I *said* I would help you. Now do you want my help or not?"

Case closed. "Okay, okay. . . . Can I do that?" Hallie asked.

"This?"

"Saw, I mean."

"Wait, Hallie. In a few minutes you can help."

"I'll go change."

Even upstairs she could hear the *zzz-hh, zzz-hh, zzz-hh* of the saw. Hallie had forgotten how much she actually liked being in her father's workshop, surrounded by hammers and wrenches, tiny jars of nails, and the dusty smell of wood shavings. She tried thinking of that as she descended the steps to the basement. She watched a minute.

"Hey, Dad, maybe we could make the base a different shape. Like an octagon or something."

"This isn't for art class, Hallie. Besides, I've already got the pieces cut. Hold this, right like that, while I drive a nail." *Bam-bam-bam.* Hallie flinched with each blow of the hammer. "I said *hold* it." *Bam-bam-bam* again. "Never mind. Get that carton over there—see it? And brush all these shavings into the box."

"What are you saving these for?" No answer. He was wrapping wire around a pencil.

"I could wind that coil around, Dad."

"It has to be a certain way for this thing to work."

In spite of herself, she protested, "Dad, this is *my* project, don't forget."

"Do you want my help or not?" he repeated. Sharper this time.

Hallie bit her lip and watched him cut a metal strip from an old can, denting it at one end with a nail. *Bam.* "Hand me those pliers, would you?"

"Can't I do anything . . . ," she began.

"What do you mean, 'do anything'?"

"Well, like with Shelley, you always let her help. You don't trust that I'll do it right."

"That's ridiculous. You're helping, same as Shelley."

"It's not the same, Dad. You won't help me when it's my idea, but if it's Shelley's, or yours . . . Whenever I'm around, you're always in a bad mood. And you never want to do things together anymore."

"Hallie, we *are* doing something together. Right now." He secured a second strip of metal to the base. *Bam.*

"No, Dad. *You're* doing it. *I'm* just watching you."

"All right, you want to do it? Fine," he bellowed. He lifted the pencil, discarding the wire coil as if it were a mere straw wrapper, then snapped it in two over his knee.

"Dad!"

"Have it your way." He tore off the magnets and hurled them deliberately into the trash can.

Hallie drew in her breath. "Dad, don't!"

Glaring, he picked up the base and smashed it upside down on the table, crushing the metal strips to a tin pancake.

"Dad! Please!" He stormed into the garage, slamming the basement door behind him with a small thunderclap.

"Hallie?" her mother called from the top of the stairs.

"I didn't . . ."

"Hallie, Crane's here."

10

"Crane?" Hallie took the stairs at a run.

"Yes, Crane. That boy from high school."

"I *know* who he is, Mom." *What if he heard?*

"He's in the living room."

Hallie's mother followed her down the hall. Crane stood up, tucking in the back of his shirt. "Hi, Hallie. I hope it's okay I—"

"Hallie, Crane was just telling me about his younger brother—Patrick, is it? You never mentioned that the boy is deaf."

I've hardly mentioned Crane. "I didn't know it myself, Mom. Mom's a social worker, and some of the kids at her agency are deaf," Hallie explained.

"Yeah, she was telling me."

"Crane knows sign language, Hallie. Even though his brother can hear some sounds, he still speaks in sign."

"That's great, Mom." Hallie opened her eyes wide, signaling *you can go now* to her mother.

"Well." Her mother paused, wringing her hands. "I still have some paperwork to finish up for tomorrow. May I fix you two some Cokes?"

"Thanks, Mom."

"Crane?"

"Sure, that'd be great, Mrs. O'Shea."

"Sorry about Mom," Hallie said in a low voice. "I didn't know you were here or I would have come up sooner."

"It's okay. I haven't been here long. I just thought I'd bring the mice stuff by. I found the design for the maze, too!"

"Oh, Crane," Hallie said, her mouth quivery. She thought she might cry. "I'm not . . . It's not . . . ," she stammered, not knowing how to tell Crane that she wouldn't be needing his supplies after he had gone to so much trouble.

"Hey, Hallie, are you okay? What's wrong?"

"Nothing. It's only . . ."

"Hey, I'm sorry. I know I should have called first. I just thought . . ."

"No, it's not you. It's . . . everything." It was like choosing the first piece of a jigsaw puzzle. Hallie didn't know where to begin.

"Should I go? I mean, I don't have to stay."

"No, don't go. Sorry. It's stupid anyway."

"What?"

Hallie launched into the story, concluding with, "Then he just blew up and smashed the whole thing."

"Oh no." Crane was quiet.

"Look, I feel bad that you brought everything all the way over here for nothing." She tried to fill the silence. "Now I don't know what I'll do."

"Look, Hallie, it wasn't you. I mean, sometimes parents do things for their own reasons. It doesn't make sense half the time, but I know mine can be the same way about stuff. Well, you know . . ."

"I guess. It's just . . . He's so angry! And I never know what he's thinking. He's always off somewhere else. I can't explain it, really. I wish I could understand what's happened to him."

"You mean he's in his own world? Where it's just him and no one else?"

"Exactly. He doesn't listen. Or even see me. Sometimes I feel invisible to him. Like he could reach out his hand and it would go right through me."

"Well, look at it this way. My dad knows I exist . . . as soon as it's time to rake leaves or work around the house," Crane joked. "And no matter what, he always knows where to find me. I swear, sometimes I think the man has radar."

Hallie's mother brought the drinks in and set them on a magazine. "Thanks, Mrs. O'Shea," Crane said.

"Shelley called earlier, Hallie."

"She's not calling tonight, then? I wanted to talk."

"She'll be home Friday, honey. She's found someone who'll be driving back to Pittsburgh, and she can get a ride."

Hallie could have hugged her mother. "That's great, Mom."

"We'll have to get some chipped ham," her mother said, thinking aloud.

"And Klondikes, don't forget. Crispy. Those are my sister's two favorite foods," Hallie explained to Crane. "She says the food at college is terrible."

"My brother says the same thing. Mystery meat, he calls it."

"Well, Hallie. I'll leave you two be," her mother said.

Hallie sipped her Coke, trying not to think any longer of the scene with her father. She glanced around: dust cobwebs clung to the ceiling corners, and the coffee table was scarred where she had carved her name at six, then tried to scratch it out. Suddenly she laughed, spitting ice back into her glass.

"What's so funny?" Crane asked.

"I was just thinking, whatever you said to Mom, you must really rate, because she never lets us bring drinks in here."

Crane raised a mischievous eyebrow. "I better finish this before I spill it, now that you've told me." He downed the rest of his glassful with a single gulp. "I should be going. Look, just keep the mice stuff for now. Maybe you can still figure something out. Um . . . I'm working after school tomorrow. Will you be on the first bus?"

"I'll be there. Thanks, Crane."

Crane touched his fingertips to his chin, signing a word.

"What does that mean? 'You're welcome'?"

"No, 'good.'"

"Good? As in, this Coke tastes good, you mean?"

"No, good as in, good you'll be on the bus with me." Crane laughed.

"I was only teasing yesterday about how you talk with your hands. I didn't realize you knew sign language."

"Well, it's usually only around my brother that I sign. But I'll show you my favorite, if you want."

Hallie nodded. He made a fist, held out his thumb and little finger, and moved it out from his chest, back and forth, back and forth, pointing toward Hallie.

"What's that one?"

"It means 'same.' But if I do it three times, like this, same same same, then it means, 'I know what you mean' or 'I feel the same as you do.'"

Hallie tried it. "Same same same. That's neat."

"I like it because it's hard to come up with the right words sometimes."

"Hey, I know that feeling."

"See? Same same same."

11

"Shelley! You're home!" Hallie mouthed through the screen door, engineering it open with her elbow while balancing books, a bag, and a box. "Hold the door, would you? Dad here?"

"He just pulled around in back. Why? Hey, aren't you even going to say welcome home?" Shelley asked.

"Please, Shelley. Just help me hide this thing, would you? Here—back behind the piano. Before Dad sees. Okay, good."

"What's in there, Hallie?"

Hallie put her finger to her lips. "Shhh! Mice."

"Mice! In that box? Whose are they?"

"He's coming up the stairs. Let's go. Just act normal."

"Hi, Dad!" Shelley called, opening the door to the basement. "Mmm," she murmured, squeezing him in a big hug when he reached the top step. Hallie hung back, forgetting the mice. She imagined her arms around her father, just like Shelley's.

"So, how's the brains of the family? Let me look at you," he said, holding her at arm's length. "You've lost some weight, haven't you?"

"What is this, a conspiracy? That's exactly what Mom said. I guess all that millet we get at school just doesn't cut it," Shelley said.

Their father laughed.

"Millet? What's millet?" Hallie asked.

"Birdseed."

"You sure don't eat like a bird!" Hallie nudged her sister with an elbow.

"Oh, Hallie."

"So, tell me. . . ." Her father wrapped an arm around Shelley's shoulders, steering her into the den. "How's the, uh, philosophy going?"

"Not philosophy, Dad. Psychology. Not as hard as calculus and English lit. Oh, and geology. My geology professor's crazy. He does stuff like bring this Slinky to class every day, right? And he has this whole theory about earthquakes he calls the Slinky principle. It's hysterical."

"So that's what they teach at college," her father teased. "I went to college, too, you know. . . ."

"I know, I know. To pick up Mom, right? Very funny. I've heard that one only a million times, Dad."

Hallie stood in the doorway to the den, framed by empty space—not entering the room, not leaving it. Their banter faded to background noise. In her excitement about college, Shelley certainly appeared to have forgotten any past anger toward her father. And he had gone from grizzly to teddy bear in the blink of an eye.

I   I   I   I   I

Shelley's first night at home. Talk of roommates and coffee drinking, exams and all-nighters filled the room, interspersed with her parents' laughter. Shelley glided through dinnertime like a skater on ice, never noticing the cold. Hallie fidgeted in her chair, folding and unfolding her legs, the ridges of the seat imprinted on her skin. She longed for a minute alone with her sister.

Finally, Shelley offered to dry the dishes. "Shelley, I need your help." Hallie lowered her voice. "You know, with the mice."

"What is it with these mysterious mice?" Shelley asked.

"Not so loud! He'll hear!"

"Dad won't care. Mom's the one who'd freak. What are you so worried about?"

"You don't know, Shelley. It all started because he wanted to build a motor. For my science project."

"So what else is new?"

"I know, but he was almost finished with one, then he had to build *another* one." Hallie lowered her voice to a whisper. "He smashed it the first time."

"What do you mean, smashed it?" Shelley asked, stopping in midswipe.

"Shhh!" Hallie glanced over her shoulder at the doorway. "I mean smashed it. Tore it apart and flattened it because I said I wanted to do the mice and he wasn't letting me help. Then he spent days getting the second one to work."

"Well, he made up for it."

"Wait, Shelley. That's not all. It was due today, and I didn't even turn it in. And he knows it. I couldn't pretend that motor was mine when I didn't do one thing on it."

"What did you tell your teacher?"

"Nothing," Hallie admitted. "Are you kidding? It's Miss Cabussi! I just handed in the mice project instead."

"Well, how'd you get the mice without their knowing?"

"Jude and I bought them at the pet store and hid them at her house all week, until today when I took them all to school."

"All? How many are there?"

"There *were* two, but they had a whole mess of babies."

"Babies! Oh, Hallie, only you could—"

"You should see them. They're cute! They look like teeny little pink piglets. Only thing is, they eat the babies, Jude said!"

"Hallie, that's gross."

"I know. I have to do something. Look, I can hide them in my closet tonight, but I need you to drive me to the pet store tomorrow morning. First thing."

"I don't get it, Hallie. You make everything so hard for yourself. Why didn't you just hand in the motor and make Dad happy for once?"

"*Nothing* makes him happy. He might act fine around you, but he hasn't said two words to me. Couldn't you even tell?"

"You exaggerate."

"Well, all I can say is it's a good thing you're here, Shelley. That's what's saving me right now."

"Girls!" Hallie's mother stood in the doorway and clapped her hands together. "Now that we have Shelley home, why don't we all four play Scrabble?"

Scrabble? Hallie couldn't believe it. Her mother beamed as if she had just arranged a free family trip to Hawaii.

"Sure, why not? The dishes are finished," Shelley agreed. "We can have teams, the way we always used to. Me and Hallie against you and Dad. Let's play right here."

"Not in the kitchen. Too gloomy in here. I don't like to look at these walls. I've been after your father to paint them for two years. You girls locate the board, and I'll set up a card table in the living room."

"You mean Dad's really going to play?" Hallie asked.

Her mother's bright expression collapsed. "I wish you would stop being so critical of your father, Hallie. Can't you see he's trying?"

"Okay, okay," Hallie said, hands up in the air, surrendering. "Don't look at me. I like Scrabble. I'm just surprised Dad wants to play, that's all."

Before she knew it, the four of them were seated around the card table as if Shelley had never left home.

"Your turn, Hallie," her mother said. "Better pay attention. . . . Your father and I are twelve points ahead, you know. Too bad we're not playing for money."

Hallie studied the board. "C'mon, Hal, we can still catch up. Let's get a really good word this time. You know, something like *xylophone* . . . or *zephyr*," Shelley said.

"Ha! Look at that. Five letters. Eight points." Their father snapped each letter into place on the board.

"Dad, it's not your turn," Hallie told him.

"Keep an eye on him, girls. I'm going to fix us some popcorn."

"Mom, we just ate dinner!"

"That was more than an hour ago, Shelley. We can't play properly without popcorn."

"Dad! There is no such word as *mungo*," Hallie argued.

"Sure there is. Haven't you heard of Marvin the Mungo Monger?"

"Marvin the what?" she and Shelley asked.

"Mungo monger. That's what we called him. Scrap metal. Marvin was always selling scrap."

"Ironworker, right?" Shelley said.

"We were on a wrecking job together, fell six floors."

"You fell six floors, Dad?" Hallie asked. "I never knew that!"

"Landed on bags of asbestos. I caught a brace on the way down, shattered my jaw. But old Marvin, he wasn't so lucky. Snapped his neck, and it was over. Just like that. He was a good ironworker. . . . You know, I never learned his real name." Her father glanced over at her. "Don't believe me? Look it up."

"I believe you," Hallie said.

He shook his head. "Always hated wrecking work."

"You couldn't get me to climb up that high," Shelley said.

"At least it's exciting," said Hallie.

"Exciting, huh!" Dad snorted. "Nobody gives a hoot when something goes up. But tear it down, and it's a regular carnival."

Hallie rearranged her letters. "I used to want to be an ironworker."

Her father laughed. "Don't let your mother hear you say that."

"Say what?" her mother asked as she carried in the popcorn.

"I was only in second grade. I remember Sister Mary Jane made us stand up and tell the class what we wanted to be when we grew up. When I announced that I wanted to be an ironworker, all the kids laughed, and Frank Pearl said, 'Hallie wants to iron clothes all day.'"

"What did you do?" Shelley asked.

"I said, 'Frank Pearl, you are so stupid,' the way you always did to me!"

"I did not. Did I?"

"Then I told everyone it meant building bridges. And in church the same day, I prayed for that boy to get swallowed up by a big ugly troll."

"Honestly, Hallie, the things you remember," her mother remarked. "Now whose turn is it?"

No one answered. The nice, neat rows of letters were crooked now. Hallie's father did not seem to hear, to notice. His gaze was far away, as if he had gone into another room. Remembering, too.

12

Hallie woke Saturday morning to apricot sunlight streaming through her windows. A perfect day for a walk, but she'd had to turn Crane down.

Sliding her clothes to one side, Hallie checked on the mice at the back of her closet. They had shredded the inside of the cardboard box, trying to tunnel their way out. *What time does the pet store open?* she wondered, tiptoeing past Shelley's room, knowing her sister rivaled Rip van Winkle when it came to sleeping.

The first one up, Hallie cracked open the front door to retrieve the paper. The note caught her eye, peeking from the old milk box on the front stoop, a long-forgotten hiding place for messages from Jude. *Must be about the mice,* Hallie thought. She stepped one bare foot onto the cool concrete and flinched with the surprise of a first toe dipped in a rushing stream. It wasn't Jude's handwriting.

Dear Hallie,
   I've had my eye on this all winter. It doesn't look as if the birds will use it again, so I thought you

61

might like it. (Don't worry—I rode my bike.) When I climbed the old pine to get it down for you, look what was inside!

The earth smells so good this morning. I wish we were taking a walk. Hope you're laughing. . . .

Happy spring!
Crane

Hallie balanced the nest in the palm of her hand, carefully examining the pale robin's egg. She turned it over and over between her fingers. So delicate that she was afraid to breathe. She tried to see inside the translucent shell, to glimpse the baby bird that had never hatched, but the egg appeared hollow, feather light.

Hallie's bookshelves were covered with seashells and driftwood, pressed leaves and dried violets. She rearranged them now, with the certainty of setting a table, and made the nest the centerpiece. She studied Crane's note, his handwriting. Printing, really— like a grade-schooler's. Sinking back on her bed, Hallie held the note to her face, closing her eyes, inhaling the ink. The paper felt sticky and smelled of pitch pine. In her mind's eye, she pictured Crane in the top of that tree and smiled to herself.

She longed for the chance to tell her sister about him. Crane. She liked hearing his name spoken aloud. And Shelley knew Crane's older brother, too. When she and Shelley went to the pet store alone, without her parents, she would mention him. She hoped Shelley wouldn't sleep until noon.

On impulse, Hallie tried sketching the nest in pencil on some old loose-leaf. She found herself erasing, starting over several times, sharpening her pencil again and again.

The nest looked so empty by itself on the page. Lonely. Should she draw the egg inside it? A still life with seashells and leaves around it? A baby bird newly hatched? She examined the drawing left and right, trying to decide, when she heard her mother call, "Breakfast! Hal-lie! Shel-ley!" from downstairs.

All through breakfast, Shelley and her mother composed a shopping list, discussing deodorant and dental floss with the fervor of political debate. They scheduled several stops and planned to make a day of it, Hallie could tell.

"Shelley," Hallie said, clenching her teeth, widening her eyes.

"I need stuff for school," Shelley said, shrugging her shoulders. "We won't be gone all day."

"Why not come with us, Hallie? We'll have lunch at Kaufmann's later on."

"Thanks, Mom, but you know how I am about shopping." Shopping quickly bored her, the way she lost interest in cereal before reaching the bottom of the bowl. "Besides, I have *things to do,*" she said, glaring at her sister. "For school."

Hallie went back upstairs to her sketch, fuming. She'd have to manage the mice on her own if Shelley didn't return on time, and the pet store was over a half hour's walk.

"You have a long weekend, honey," her mother said, continuing the conversation as she entered Hallie's room. Hallie shoved the unfinished drawing inside her desk. "I hate to see you here by yourself all day."

"I know, Mom, but this is really important."

"Well, your father'll be downstairs if you need anything." Her mother slid open one side of the closet door on its rollers. Hallie leaped from her chair. "Mom! What are you doing?"

Her mother pulled out a skirt, lingered, apparently checking for spots. "Getting a few work things. I have to stop at the cleaners."

"You won't have time, will you?" Hallie asked, wishing her gone. *Please be quiet, mice. Do not move. Do not make a sound.* "Here, let me help you," Hallie offered, yanking out clothes, purposely making the hangers screech.

"Not that one, Hallie. Here, give me these and put this back. Close that closet door, would you?" Hangers in hand, her mother left the room.

Restless, Hallie gazed out the window, made her bed, went downstairs, tried calling Jude, glanced at the funnies, stared into the cookie drawer, climbed the steps, fed the mice, tried Jude again, read some of *The Call of the Wild.*

> And closely akin to the visions of the hairy man was the call still sounding in the depths of the forest. It filled him with a great unrest and strange desires. It caused him to feel a vague, sweet gladness, and he was aware of wild yearnings for he knew not what.

When she couldn't read anymore, could no longer

sit still, she paced the length of her room, checked her watch for the third time in fifteen minutes.

Her stomach growled. She was nearly always hungry. She imagined the lunch Shelley and her mother would have eaten as she studied the refrigerator. Nothing. In the middle of coating a piece of bread with peanut butter, she set the knife down.

"Dad?" she called. The rhythmic striking of metal against metal vibrated through the basement. Halfway down the steps, she called again. Then, "Dad!" a third time, from the doorway to the garage.

He was shaping a blackened piece of metal, holding it at one end with tongs. "What is it, Hallie?"

"Want a sandwich? I mean, I'm making some. Peanut butter. I could make you one. With jelly or something."

"Not right now."

"You didn't stop for lunch all day, Dad. It's almost four."

"How about bologna, then? With mayonnaise?"

"I'll look. I don't know if . . . Well, I'll check."

Hallie downed her peanut butter with a glass of milk while she fixed the bologna for her father. She smothered a second slice of bread for herself and carried both sandwiches downstairs.

Sparks flew from her father's burning torch. Blasts of white smoke engulfed him.

"Don't stand so close, Hallie. Or you'll have to put on goggles."

"Don't you want this?" Hallie asked, offering the plate.

"In a minute. Just set it down."

Hallie stepped back, bit into her sandwich, worked the peanut butter from the roof of her mouth. She asked the question that had been festering inside her. "*Is* that a sculpture, Dad? I mean, what is it?"

The sparks stopped. Smoke settled. He set the torch down. "What does it look like to you?"

Hallie wasn't sure what to say. She feared she might guess the wrong thing. It looked like flying pieces of twisted metal to her. *A snake?* She didn't think it was a snake.

"Birds, maybe? I don't know. . . ."

"It's not so much *what* it is, Hallie. It's what I'm trying to do."

Hallie persisted. "What are you trying to do?"

"People think of metal as cold—all sharp angles and edges. I'm trying to make it flow. Show movement with curves and crescents, not lines."

"You mean like a mobile?"

He tore a bite out of the sandwich, chewing vehemently. "Not really. It'll be stationary. But parts of it can move. That will help with the idea of something more fluid, you know, like water."

"So it's more a birdbath then, or something?"

Her father became animated. "You have to think of it as a concept, Hallie. Not just a structure with a function. An art, not just a science." He wolfed down another bite, walking around the piece, pointing to various shapes and spirals of welded steel, gesturing with the half-eaten sandwich.

Hallie tried to concentrate, strained to understand. Her father so rarely spoke excitedly about anything . . . but it was getting late and she hadn't done a thing about the pet store.

Finally, she interjected, "I've got to go, Dad," hating to end the conversation. "I'll take the plates up."

He stopped in midsentence, deflated. "Here." He tossed the remnants of the sandwich back onto the plate, the white bread now fingerprinted with black.

"I'm not just saying . . . I mean, I've really got to be somewhere. By five."

One flip of the hood and he became a comic-book villain, a bug-eyed alien behind glass. "Well, thanks for showing me," she said to the man behind the face shield.

"Thanks for stopping by" came his muffled response.

Hallie raced up the two flights of stairs. *Stopping by?* She haphazardly secured the box of mice in the bottom of her backpack and set off at a half-run for Pet World.

"Hey, Hallie, you still want to take those mice back? We'll have to hurry."

"Never mind, Shelley. I already walked them back. The pet store's closed now anyway."

"Oh, well, I better finish getting ready then."

"Ready for what? Where're you going?"

"Out," Shelley answered.

"Who with?"

"Just some people. Denise and everybody."

"Can I come?"

"No."

"Aw, Shelley . . ."

"Look, you know you wouldn't have a good time anyway. Besides, I never get to see my friends."

"Huh! You never get to see your sister either." Hallie followed her to the bathroom mirror three times and back again. She wanted a chance to talk to Shelley—really talk. About their father. More than some whispered conversation.

"We have all week. We'll do something another night, I promise."

"Maybe we can still play Scrabble. All of us again. You know, after you come home."

"I don't think so. I'll be out late."

"When will *we* get to do something, Shelley? I mean, just us?"

"What are you, Hallie, my shadow? Out of my room," she said, pushing the door shut. "I'm late already."

A sweet trail of Narcissus lingered in the hall after Shelley had gone. Hallie's stomach did a flip-flop as she sneaked back into her sister's room, soundlessly locking the door behind her. She watched as the car backed out of the driveway. Only then did she turn on the light. The room was chilly and smelled of stale sweat. Hallie waded through clothes littering the floor. The perfume bottle was not on the dresser.

Shelley's suitcase lay gaping on the unmade bed, spilling out dirty socks, underwear, inside-out shirts and sweaters. Hallie's eye zoomed in on a zippered pouch. *Maybe it's in here,* she told herself, unzipping the pocket, checking behind her, watching the doorknob to make sure it didn't turn. Bobby pins, tampons, bunched-up nylons. Bottles, jars, and tubes of makeup with names like base and liner.

Fascinated, Hallie unscrewed the lids, setting bottle after bottle on the desk top, smelling each one. There was the perfume; she dabbed some behind her ears, at her wrists, as she had seen Shelley do. She opened the compact with the tiny mirror inside and sneezed.

She found two colors of blush—Whispering Orchid and Pretty-in-Peach. Hallie rubbed two round spots, one kind on each cheek. Then she twisted the thin brush from the mascara tube and caked it on her eyelashes. Blinking became a chore.

Pulling at her eyelashes with one hand, with the other she returned the compact and mascara to their place. A bit of red stuck out like a flag from behind a pair of stockings. Cigarettes! Dislodging the pack, she pulled one out, running it underneath her nose. *Shelley doesn't even smoke!* Hallie thought, brushing crumbs of rich-smelling tobacco from her lap. *At least I've never seen her.*

Hallie leaned over to shut the window, then stopped herself. *She must smoke in her room with the window open so Mom and Dad won't find out.* She tried to digest this terrible secret. *When did*

Shelley start smoking anyway? Why did she? How come she never told me? Suddenly, she wanted out of that room, back in the safety of her own.

She replaced the cigarette in its soft package and couldn't help but notice a wad of paper tucked into the cellophane. *You shouldn't look at it,* a voice inside her whispered. SIGN YOUR NAME HERE IF YOU READ THIS, Shelley's childhood diary had always warned on the first page. Hallie half expected to find a similar message for intruders here. She unfolded the paper.

It was Shelley's handwriting, all right. Hallie scanned the page:

The darkness perches on the sill, leans against the window, presses on the pane. The blackness beckons, stark and secret. Even the moon casts shadows that slip in through the cracks. Shadows surround me.

I have opened my window to let in the night. I am a stranger to this room. I did not ask to come here. Familiarity tugs at me like the tide, and I fight it, only to sink into uncertainty.

A thousand nights take me back to the hill where we watched the moon. Where are you now? Things are always so different in the morning, in the light, as if the night never happened.

Didn't Shelley want to come home? And what was this, these words about night and darkness? An essay for school? It couldn't be, not tucked away in there. A love letter? Surely not. Shelley didn't even have a boyfriend. At least not one that Hallie knew of.

What was happening? Shelley had always been the

kind of person who wouldn't notice the moon unless someone told her to look up. Hallie quickly refolded the paper, replaced the cigarettes, stuffed the nylons around them, closed the pouch, shut out the light. *Oh no, the makeup!* Light on again. She gathered together the assortment of eye shadow, face cream, and lip gloss, accidentally tipping over the Narcissus. Squinting one eye, she was relieved to see a bit left in the bottle. She grabbed a pair of underwear and swabbed the tiny puddle, leaving behind a small white cloud on the desk.

Safe in her own room, Hallie went to the mirror above her dresser. Inky streaks ran down the face in the reflection, ruining the rosy circles of Whispering Orchid and Pretty-in-Peach.

13

Jude followed Hallie onto the bus after school, lugging her trombone behind her. "No band today, Jude?"

"For once. Mr. Maris was out sick. I guess he decided to extend his Easter vacation."

Hallie was glad to have the company. Her entire break seemed to have been spent waiting for Shelley to come home or to get off the phone. When they reached the manhole, she asked, "Why don't you come over? Maybe we can talk Shelley into driving us to get ice cream."

"Do you think so?"

"Well, it's a *big* maybe. You never know with Shelley." Hallie's surreptitious discovery put Shelley in a different light now, this girl who secretly smoked cigarettes and wrote about the night. And had so little time, suddenly, for Hallie.

Shelley wasn't home at first. Then Hallie and Jude were making sandwiches in the kitchen when they heard Hallie's father yelling, "I said three o'clock. When I say three, I mean three! You're in my house now, Shelley. This isn't college."

"I said I'm sorry, Dad. Geez."

"Well, Shelley's back," Hallie told Jude. "But so much for her driving us anywhere." They went upstairs to Hallie's room, balancing plates and glasses of milk.

"Hey, Jude, how's it going?" Shelley came in, plopped herself on the bed. "Hey, Jude—get it?" Hallie and Jude just looked at each other. "Okay, old joke. You know, Dad nearly bit my head off just now, Hallie. I'm not *that* late. What's the big deal?"

"Who knows?" Hallie could not begin explaining her father's mysterious trips to the bridge when she didn't even understand them herself. "I told you, he just gets that way lately."

"Guess I caught him in a bad mood," Shelley said.

"He'll get over it," Jude offered. "My dad acts mad at me one minute, and the next he's as sweet as Santa Claus."

"Yeah, Dad's been in a bad mood for the last three months straight!" Hallie joked. It felt good, the three of them laughing together. Even the shadow of her father's moods looming over her seemed less dark.

"Looks like you're stuck with us, Shel."

"Yeah. Won't be going anywhere for a while. Unless it's on foot." They laughed again.

Shelley brought in pictures of her campus and dorm room for Hallie and Jude to see. "It's a mess!" Hallie screeched. Clothes, papers, and books were dumped everywhere. "How can you find your own bed?"

"That's just my side of the room."

"You better not show these to Mom."

"I know. What I can't figure out is why everybody hangs out in our room to study."

"Maybe they like pigpens," Hallie suggested.

"Now you're starting to sound like my dad," Jude said. "It must be great not having someone telling you to clean up your room before you're allowed to go anywhere."

"My roommate tells me that anyway. I just threaten to tell her boyfriend that she wears her shower cap when she studies. And uses toe separators. Tapes plastic bags around her feet at night."

"You're kidding!" Jude and Hallie laughed.

When they were finished with the pictures, Shelley looked around the room as if seeing it for the first time. "Your room looks different."

"No, it's the same. You've just been away."

"It's funny how that is," Shelley mused. She nodded toward the shelves. "Some things haven't changed."

"Why do you collect this junk?" Jude asked. She picked up an open mussel shell, still hinged like a butterfly's wings. "Whew! This stinks!" She nearly dropped it back on the shelf. Then she homed in on the bird's nest. "Like this thing. What do you want with a hunk of mud and sticks anyway?"

"Hey, put that down, Jude," Hallie cried. "I didn't *collect* it. Someone gave it to me."

"What for?" Shelley asked.

"I don't know what for. He just did."

"Ooh, *he*? You didn't say it was a he. Does *he* happen to have black hair, be about so tall"—Jude reached her arm up over her head—"and go to the high school?"

"High school! You didn't tell me you had a *boy*friend, Hallie," Shelley said. "So what's this guy's name?"

"Cra-ane," Jude teased, fluttering her eyelids.

"Oh, so that's whose name I saw written on the bathroom mirror. In the steam, with a big heart around it," Shelley informed Jude.

"You did not!"

"That's him all right. Big spender, too," Jude joked, indicating the nest. "Hey, maybe this is supposed to be a *love* nest." Shelley and Jude got a good laugh over that.

"Ha. Ha. You think you're so funny. Just shut up, you guys. He's not . . . Hey, give me that!" Jude was holding the egg now. Hallie reached to snatch it from her.

"Shelley, catch!" Jude threw the egg across the room to Shelley, who caught it between her hands. Hallie didn't actually hear the crunch, only the clap of Shelley's hands. When she opened them, Hallie saw the remnants of that perfect little egg, so fragile, shattered into tiny pieces in her sister's palm.

Jude looked sheepish. "Oops."

Shelley began, "Hallie, we didn't mean . . ."

"I can't believe you guys are so mean. You're always ganging up on me. Everybody is so mean to me. Why don't you just go back to college if you love it so much?" Hallie yelled at Shelley. "See if I care." She grabbed a pillow and flung it against the wall, knocking askew the Alice in Wonderland drawing she had done in art class.

"Geez-oh-man, Hallie. It's only an egg," Jude said. "I don't see what the big deal is."

"No, you wouldn't. Forget it, Jude. Just leave me alone." She buried her face in the other pillow.

"We can go into my room, Jude," Shelley offered.

"No, I better get home anyway. C'mon, Hallie, I'm sorry." Silence. "Well, I guess I'll be leaving, then."

"I'll be in my room if you want to talk, okay, Hal?" Shelley half asked. Hallie did not say a word. She heard them whispering in the hall, then the sound of Jude on the stairs. Leaving. The ghosts of her footsteps lingering there.

Shelley left for college again. On her last morning home, she asked, "Are you still mad, Hallie?"

"No," Hallie said, her eyes boring a hole in the carpet.

"Please don't be mad at me anymore."

"I said I'm not."

"What's wrong, then?"

"You were almost never home. Not even on Easter! We hardly got to talk the whole time. Now you're leaving again."

"What do you mean? Sure we talked."

"I mean about Dad and stuff."

"Okay, what about him?"

"Shelley, you know what I mean. You saw what he's like."

"C'mon, Hallie. Everyone's entitled to a bad mood now and then."

"It's different, Shelley. I mean it. You don't know because you're not here."

"Hallie, you just think he's different, so you act different. You act like you're afraid of him or something. It's just Dad. He'll probably go back to work again, and everything will be fine. Okay?"

"I guess," Hallie answered. But she hardly believed it.

Their father honked the horn in the driveway. "Got to go. Dad's driving me downtown to catch my ride back to Michigan. Here, Hallie, can you carry this downstairs for me?"

The words from Shelley's note echoed inside her head as Hallie waved good-bye to her sister. *The miles will separate us now, but I promise you they will never change things. . . .*

She didn't keep her promise, Hallie thought as the car pulled away. She missed Crane. He was the only one left to talk to.

"So how was the flower show?" Hallie tried asking Jude at school. She wanted her friend to know she was no longer angry about the egg.

"Don't even ask," Jude said, as if nothing had happened between them. "I'm just glad you're not mad."

"I'm sorry, Jude. Really I am."

"Me, too. Hey, consider yourself lucky you *weren't* speaking to me, or I might have conned you into coming with us."

"That bad, huh? What happened?"

"Okay, well, for starters I had to ride on the hump in the middle of the front seat the whole way, with all the cousins. We drove around half the morning looking for a place to park, then Jessie blows this enormous bubble, right? The thing pops right in her eye and she can't open it. Stuck like glue. We go find ice and we can't get it off, so we have to drive to some medical place. She wailed the entire time. I mean wailed. I didn't go in, it was so embarrassing, so I wait for like an hour in the car. Then, after all that, we finally get there, and there are six tulips. Count them—six. And they call it a tulip festival."

"What a disaster."

"You're not kidding. But there's more, Hal. . . . Crane was there and—"

"You saw *Crane*? At the shower flow?"

"No, at the flower show," Jude corrected. "Well, actually, they saw me."

"Crane *Henderson*?"

"Yes, Crane Henderson. How many Cranes do you know?"

"Are you positive? I don't see how he could have been. I mean, he said he had to work all day Saturday. He even asked me to go downtown with him next Saturday, since he was working this—"

"Look, I wasn't going to tell you. . . . I mean, I didn't want to get you any more upset, but then when I saw him with Darlene . . ."

"Dar*lene*? Darlene *Shramm*?" Hallie had called Crane on Saturday night, then again on Sunday. Each time his mother had said, "He can't come to the phone right now." Hallie had dismissed it, thinking she had called during their quiet time. Now she wasn't so sure.

So what if he went to the flower show with Darlene, she told herself. *But then he lied about having to work. And Darlene's in ninth grade,* another voice answered. *So? Well, maybe he really likes her. What made you think he liked you anyway? Just you?*

"Well, so what?" Hallie said aloud. "I mean, it's not like . . . You make it seem like it's some big thing all the time," she said accusingly.

"Me? What did I do? Look, Hal, I know how much you like the guy. Why can't you just admit it for once? So what if you do. What's wrong with that?"

"Nothing. I do like him. It's just . . . I don't know. I can't explain it, Jude. We have such a good time doing stuff together, and we talk, but you make it seem . . . I mean, it's not like that."

"Oh, so you mean if Darlene is his *girl*friend, you don't care?"

"No, I care, but . . . I don't know."

"Well, if I were you, I'd sure find out."

"What do you mean?"

It was Jude who concocted the scheme. Hallie gasped at first, but here she was, walking down Thompson Run Road with her friend as easily as if they went to Shramm's Farm every day.

"What do we do if someone sees us?" she asked Jude.

"Don't worry. No one'll see us. We'll just pretend we came to buy eggs or something."

"Since when do we get eggs from Shramm's Dairy?"

"Since now," Jude told her. Hallie couldn't help laughing.

"What if Crane's there?"

"That's the point, isn't it?"

"Yeah, but I mean, what if he sees us?"

"Hallie, take it easy. We'll think of something." Jude stopped walking a moment to think. "I know. If anybody asks, tell them my dad has heart trouble, and we heard their eggs are low in cholesterol."

"Is there such a thing? Do you think anyone would believe us?"

"Sure, why not?"

Hallie wasn't so sure, but she could already see the sign, SHRAMM'S FARM/DAIRY. When they reached the driveway, she said, "Hey, wait. We can't just march right up to the house!"

"Over here, into the woods," Jude said. Every leaf and twig underfoot seemed to announce their arrival.

"We should never have come here, Jude," Hallie whispered.

"I think I heard someone. Get down." Jude yanked the back of Hallie's jacket until she crouched to the ground. Off in the distance a dog barked, but there was no sign of Crane. Or Darlene.

"They must be around here someplace," Jude said, sounding certain.

"We don't even know for sure if Crane's working today."

"Well, if he is, he must not work up at the house."

"He told me he feeds the animals and cleans out the stables, wherever they are."

"I'm going to have a look. You wait here, Hallie, and keep watching for Darlene. If only one of us goes, it won't make as much noise."

"Jude, wait . . . ," Hallie protested, about to say, "This is a big place." But Jude was already slinking through the woods, bent low to the ground, skirting the dirt road that led away from the house.

Once Jude was gone, Hallie walked out of the woods and down to the faded old farmhouse. Her heart thumped as she peered through a window into a kitchen. Pots and pans and bunches of dried herbs hung from ceiling rafters.

What was it she expected—or feared—to see? Crane and Darlene talking, laughing? Drinking Cokes and doing homework together? Holding hands? Hallie pressed her face to the window, shielding her eyes from the glare. A thorn snagged her coat sleeve.

Darlene was bent over a large sink, her back to Hallie. When she stood up to stir something on the stove, Hallie saw that she wore a plastic cap with holes on her head. She watched, fascinated. One hunk at a time, Darlene carefully hooked some hair with a crochet needle, pulled it through a hole in the cap, then dipped it in a bowl on the counter.

Hallie stifled a laugh. She didn't hear the dog, or see it, until it was snapping at the hem of her jeans, snarling deep in its throat. She tried to back away, but the dog's teeth were clamped to her pant leg.

"Down, boy, down," she whispered. "Let go!" she told him, hopping on one foot while frantically trying to wrestle the other leg from the dog's grip.

The dog hung on tight. In a tug-of-war, she struggled as far as the driveway. One wild, desperate kick, and she hit the dog square on the snout. He let out a loud yelp as she jerked her leg free, ripping her pants. The dog jumped on her, pawed her, almost knocking her down. Something sharp pierced her hand.

Hallie ran—ran down the driveway and out toward the road, the dog barking and chasing after her. Someone was yelling now, yelling and whistling. "Nutmeg! Get back here!"

Hallie didn't stop to think, to check her hand, to wait for Jude. She just ran, like a criminal, as if her life depended on it—ran until the only barking she heard was imaginary.

15

"She looked like a zebra!" Jude was crying with laughter. "I wish you could have seen her, Hal. After you bolted down the driveway, Darlene was out there with half her hair sticking out in spikes, holding some cap with one hand and chasing after the dog with a towel at the same time. If Crane did like her, he's probably changed his mind by now!"

"Stop! You're making my sides hurt!" Hallie clutched her stomach, not knowing which was funnier, Jude doubled over on the front stoop of her house, or the thought of Darlene with half a head of striped hair. "You mean you were in that tree the whole time?"

"Well, I wasn't about to come down. Not with Crane and Mr. Shramm practically right under me. They heard all the barking and yelling and came running from behind the barn."

"So Crane really *was* there! Oh, Jude, what if Darlene saw me . . . you know, enough to know it was me?"

84

"Look, all she saw was somebody running in a blue jacket. Every other kid in Saint Scholastica has a jean jacket like yours. It could have been the mailman, for all they know."

"And nobody saw you either?"

"That's what took me so long. I waited until Crane left and Mr. Shramm went back inside."

"At least *you* didn't get attacked by a vicious mongrel and have to run for your life."

"Hey, I could have been caught up there. Try explaining that one. Besides, it was your brilliant idea to go snooping right in the window. That's what dogs are for, you know, to protect houses from prowlers and robbers and stuff. Let me see where you got bit anyway."

Hallie unwrapped the messy gauze around her right hand. "It's only two little puncture holes, but I wrapped it up so Mom wouldn't see what it looks like."

"Ooh, Hallie, that doesn't look so good. Does it hurt?"

"Just throbs. My whole hand feels sort of numb, though."

"Well, look at it this way. You can get out of doing homework for a while."

"Yeah, I'll just tell all my teachers the Shramms' dog bit me while I was trespassing on their property, playing Peeping Tom."

"Well, one good thing is, we found out Crane *was* working on Saturday when I saw him with Darlene. He was just getting plants for the Shramms' garden."

"I don't see how you can be so sure."

"Hallie, I was right there, even if I was up a tree. Mr. Shramm said to Crane, 'We better finish those plants you two bought before the rain hits.'"

Hallie had stopped listening. "Jude, I'm scared about getting rabies or something."

"Rabies? You don't get that from pets. Know what I mean?"

"What other kinds of dogs are there?"

"You know, like strays. I mean, if a dog has rabies, it looks all crazy and foams at the mouth and stuff. Doesn't it?"

"I don't know. All I know is that you have to get a bunch of shots and they plunge this gigantic needle in your stomach. Oh, Jude, maybe I should tell Mom. But how would I explain? And she'll ask whose dog and everything."

"Tell her you went to see Crane at work."

"But what if she mentions it to him sometime? Then he'll know it was me there."

"Look, Hallie. You can't have rabies. People don't get rabies just like that. Besides, you're not even sick or anything." Jude smiled reassuringly. "I know. Let's go ask my mom what happens if a person gets rabies."

"She's going to know somebody got bit by a dog if you ask her that."

"Well, maybe you could find out from Crane if the Shramms' dog has had its shots and everything."

"I can't start asking Crane a bunch of questions about some dog I supposedly never even saw!"

"Let's look it up. I bet the encyclopedia will have something."

Hallie followed Jude into her dad's study. Jude read aloud: "'Rabies is an infectious disease that destroys the nerve cells in parts of the brain and almost always causes . . .' Never mind that part. 'The word *rabies* is Latin for "rage" or "fury." The disease probably received its name because infected animals often become excited and attack any object or animal in their way.'"

"See? I told you!" Hallie interrupted. "That dog attacked me!"

"Yeah, but it doesn't count because you kicked it first. I'd bite back, too."

"Well, I didn't mean to."

Jude continued: "'Because one of the symptoms of rabies is an inability to swallow water, the disease is sometimes called *hydrophobia,* which means "fear of water."' There, see, you're not afraid of water."

Hallie swallowed deliberately. She thought her throat felt tight.

"'Among the first symptoms are pain, burning, or numbness at the site—'"

"Numbness? My hand does feel numb! That's exactly what I told you before. Remember?"

"Let me finish. 'The victim complains of headaches and acts extremely restless.' Yep, that's you all right."

"Jude, I mean it. . . ."

"'The throat feels full, and swallowing becomes difficult.'"

"Oh no . . ."

"Hallie, it says here you don't even feel any symptoms for ten days to seven months."

"Oh, great, so I won't even know—"

"Girls." Mrs. Jacobs stuck her head in the room. "Hallie's mother phoned and would like her to get home."

"Okay, sure. Look, I'll see you at school tomorrow, Jude. That is, if I'm still alive."

"Still alive? What's this all about?" Mrs. Jacobs asked.

"Oh, nothing. Just an expression," Hallie said, heading for the front door.

"I'll walk you to the manhole," Jude said, steering Hallie down the hall. Outside, she said, "Maybe you *better* tell your mom, Hallie. I mean, what if you should go to a doctor?"

"I don't know. Maybe you're right. She's going to ask, but . . . No, I just can't, Jude. Don't worry. I'll be okay."

When Hallie was alone in the dark of her room that night, her confidence waned. What made her go look in that window? If only she had stayed hidden in the woods! She never should have gone to Shramm's in the first place. She lay in bed, tracing and retracing the day's events in her mind, the way someone looking for a lost wallet recounts his movements step-by-step.

It didn't seem real to her now, but she had her aching hand to remind her. She could hardly look forward to spending Saturday with Crane now. Even the thought of Darlene's striped hair was little consolation. Hallie closed her eyes, willing herself to sleep. It was no use. Each time she dozed, she would awaken, only to reach for the glass of water on her bedside table and try swallowing again and again.

16

"You were in my dream the other night," Crane told Hallie on the bus ride downtown.

"Me? Really?"

"Yes, really. All I remember is you were walking out to this mailbox to get a letter or something, but when you put your hand in, you got stung by a bee. Then I helped you pull out the stinger, and we wrapped up the bee in a pink napkin and buried it. It was really weird. I mean, you know how dreams are."

"Wonder what it means," Hallie said, but she couldn't help thinking about the dog bite and feeling guilty. The secret had weighed on her all week like a coat too heavy for her shoulders, making her tired.

"I don't know. There's probably some big theory about it. But you haven't gotten any bee stings lately, have you?"

"Nope. Not lately."

"That's good. It's kind of strange about burying that bee, don't you think?" Crane asked. "Like when you're a kid and you have a pet goldfish or a turtle, you know, and it dies? Boy, we could have a whole cemetery with all the pets that died at our house. How about you?"

"Well, my mom was never too big on pets, but I had a parakeet once," Hallie told him. "I wanted it to talk so bad. I remember the day after I got it, I faked sick just to stay home from school and talk to it all day."

"Saying what?"

"Oh, you know, 'Pretty bird, pretty bird,' and 'Polly want a cracker?' Stuff like that."

"Did it talk?" Crane asked.

"No, but it sure squawked a lot. My dad used to call up the operator and put the phone next to the bird cage. That bird screeched like crazy every time. Then he'd hold his nose and say, 'Operator, operator!' in a nasal voice, like it was supposed to be the bird talking."

"You're kidding. Wow! My dad wouldn't dream of pulling a stunt like that. He thinks people should write more letters and do away with the telephone. Sometimes I think he says it just to get a rise out of us kids."

"Yeah, well, my dad wouldn't do that now. I mean, you know what I mean. I told you about the science project and everything."

"How did that go, by the way? I meant to ask you, but then your sister was here and everything."

"I got the mice. That's a story in itself. And turned in a maze, like you said. I had to cut it out of cardboard, since there wasn't much time. Thanks again— for all your stuff, I mean. It really bailed me out."

"Sure. Hey, Grant Street. Let's get off here." They stepped down onto the busy sidewalk. "What would you like to do first?"

"Um, let's see. Doughnuts," Hallie said.

"Okay, doughnuts it is. You know of any good place around here?"

"Yep."

"Lead the way."

A small bell jingled, announcing their arrival. A moist, sugary smell permeated the bakery. Thick as river fog. Hallie breathed it in slowly, remembering. "Mmm, smell that."

Crane inhaled, closing his eyes. "Mmm. I could stand to breathe that all day."

"Crane, we have to get the powdery ones. I hope they're just out of the oven—you know, the kind that melts in your mouth."

"Something tells me you've been here before," Crane teased.

"Not for a long time. I used to ride downtown every Saturday with my dad, and we always came here. He says this place has been here since he was a kid growing up on the North Side."

"Hey, want to get some hot chocolate, too?"

"You read my mind."

"We could take these down to the Point and sit by the fountain. . . ."

"Okay, let's!"

Hallie tucked her hair inside the hood of her sweatshirt. The day was cool, overcast, threatening rain, but neither of them noticed the weather. They walked past Jenkins Arcade, through Market Square, sinking their teeth in the still-warm doughnuts, looking up at the carved griffins on a building, talking over the noise of traffic. A car painted purple dragged its muffler against the street, shooting out sparks like her father's welding machine.

"Hallie, look at me. You have a powdered sugar mustache!" Crane rubbed it away with his thumb.

"You have one, too." She laughed, pointing, not touching his face.

"Let's run!" Crane said, clutching his camera to his chest, as soon as they reached the grassy area of Point State Park.

Panting, they reached the rim of the fountain. Hallie felt a fine mist tickling her face and eyelashes. "Feel that spray," she said. "Close your eyes and imagine you're on a boat."

"Or underneath a waterfall."

"Yes," Hallie whispered. They sat in silence on the ledge around the fountain and listened. When Hallie opened her eyes again, the sun was poking through just enough to make tiny rainbows shimmer where the water formed an arc. Crane kneeled, stood, bent over, turned his camera sideways, snapping pictures from different angles.

"Wait, I want to take your picture with the fountain behind you. Stay right there. No, stand on the ledge. Good. Like that." Crane took what seemed like a long time focusing his camera. Hallie squirmed, feeling self-conscious. "Hurry up so we can go ride the incline," she said.

"Hallie, look here," Crane directed. *Click. Click.* "Hold it right like that. Great!"

"Except my hair was blowing in my face."

"It looks good like that."

"Right." Hallie rolled her eyes.

"Trust me." Crane grinned. *Click.* "Okay, no more pictures. Let's make a wish, Hallie." He fished deep in his pocket. "Here's a penny. You first."

"But I have to think of what I wish."

"Okay. Me first, then. I *know* what I wish." Crane tossed his penny toward the center of the fountain.

"What?"

"Can't tell. But you can tell me yours!"

"No way! Forget it."

Hallie couldn't decide what to wish anyhow, so she tucked the penny into her pocket when Crane wasn't looking. She watched the tugs inching along, skimming past like slow turtles, pushing barges heaped with coal. The rivers, all three, snaked beneath bridges and met here, at this small spit of land where they stood.

"There're the Three Sisters," she told Crane, pointing. "See?"

"The Three Sisters?"

"Those right next to each other. The Sixth Street, Seventh, and Ninth Street bridges. See how they're built exactly alike? That's how they get their name."

"I never knew that. How about the one across there that looks like a big number eight turned sideways?" Crane said.

"That's my favorite! It's like an infinity sign."

"Yeah."

"There used to be a covered bridge there, the first bridge ever in Pittsburgh. Now it's the oldest steel bridge."

"Wow, how do you know all this stuff, Hallie?"

"My dad. He built a lot of the bridges around here. And believe me, the ones he didn't work on he knows about. Ever since I was little, he took me to see bridges and told me stories about them."

The City of Bridges. She wondered how many of these bridges her father had worked on since he was fourteen—Crane's age.

"You never told me your dad builds bridges."

"Well, he doesn't anymore. He used to."

"How come? Didn't like it?"

"Are you kidding? He loved it. That's practically all he ever thinks about still."

"How come he quit, then?"

"He didn't quit, really. They just shut down the bridge he was working on, and he couldn't find another job. A bridge job, anyway. It drives him crazy seeing that bridge just sit there. Dead. And everyone calling it the Bridge to Nowhere."

"The Bridge to Nowhere! You mean your dad *built* that bridge?"

"Well, he worked on it, yeah."

"That one there, right? With the crazy stuff written all over it. I take pictures there a lot." Crane turned, looked at Hallie. "It must be neat to have a dad who builds bridges and tells you all that stuff."

"I used to think it was great, back when he worked a job. Now I don't know." The words rushed out.

"Sometimes . . . well, he's so moody all the time. I never know when he's going to blow up over nothing. Then even when I try to guess what won't make him mad, he ends up mad anyway."

"You mean just since he doesn't have a job?"

"Yeah, but it's not just a job. I don't know, ever since he quit working on bridges, it's as if something inside him's broken. It's hard to explain. I mean, I used to love being with my dad, any chance to do things with him. Now I hardly know what to say to him." Hallie bit her lip, looked away. "I'm sorry. I didn't mean to say all this."

"Hey, it's okay. I don't mind hearing. Thanks for telling me, actually. I could show you my favorite thing there, on the bridge, if you'd like to see."

"But what about Mount Washington? I thought you wanted to ride the incline."

Crane shrugged his shoulders. "This'll be more fun. You'll see."

Hallie shivered, suddenly feeling a chill. "Are you cold?" Crane reached to take her hand. "Hey! What happened to you?" he asked when he saw the Band-Aids crisscrossing her palm.

"Oh, nothing. I, um, cut it. Doing the maze for my science project." She shivered again.

"Oh, I'm sorry. Here, let me . . ." Crane intertwined his fingers with hers. Before leaving the Point, they sat huddled a minute, warming their hands in the same pocket.

17

"Do they let people out here? I mean, what happens if you get caught?" Hallie asked Crane as they climbed over the barricade and out onto the Bridge to Nowhere. The lower deck was covered with graffiti, bold as billboards. Peace symbols, hearts, declarations of love. Huge red spray-painted letters boasting BILLY LOVES SARAH and SARAH LOVES BILLY.

"Don't worry. I don't think anybody cares. Look up there." Crane pointed, and Hallie saw DAM EVERYTHING BUT THE CIRCUS zigzagging up and down along one of the top trusses. "They didn't even spell it right." Hallie laughed. HOLD FAST TO DREAMS ran along the handrail, paint trailing from each letter of the word *dreams*.

"Look, here's what I wanted to show you, Hallie. There are poems and everything here, see?

"The water is wide
I can't cross over
And neither have
I wings to fly.

97

"Here's another one, too. Down here—look. Listen to this." Hallie kneeled next to Crane as he read:

> "Buy me some rings
> And a gun that sings
> A flute that toots
> And a bee that stings
> Strap yourself to a tree with roots
> You ain't going nowhere
>
> We'll climb that bridge
> After it's gone
> After we're way past it"

"Is that a song?" Hallie asked. "It's strange. Kind of sad."

"I know. But just think of all the different people who have come out here and remembered something, or written something."

"Yeah, and not like the graffiti at school," Hallie said.

"That's for sure. 'High school sucks' is about as intelligent as it gets there. Hey, I know," Crane said. "Want to write something ourselves?"

"What would we write?" Hallie asked.

"I don't know. Anything. Even just our names."

"But we don't have paint or a brush or anything."

"I've got a penknife," Crane said. "We could scratch our initials somewhere, if you want."

"It's okay. Go ahead if you want to."

"Never mind. Let's stretch out on our backs and look up," Crane suggested.

They stared past the lines of steel on the upper deck to the diamond-shaped cross beams laced with sky, a cathedral above their heads. The sun peered from behind the arm of a cloud. Beneath the bridge, a man practiced his saxophone. Long, plaintive notes wafted up to them, riding the breeze like the scent of summer honeysuckle.

Crane was thinking aloud. "Just imagine—up there, above the clouds, there's space. Gravity. Planets spinning around, stars, galaxies, the whole universe. And it goes on forever. I mean, we're talking *infinity*."

"It *is* amazing. How can there even be such a thing as infinity?" Hallie asked. "You know, forever and ever. No end. I don't get it."

"It's like this science fiction show I saw once. The guy never got old. He lived for hundreds of years and kept going on forever. He just never died. Then it got to the point where he would have done anything to die. Even though at the beginning he didn't want to."

"'What you think won't happen won't,'" Hallie said, quoting the fortune on the gum wrapper Crane had found on their first walk.

"Hey, you remember that?" Crane stood and leaned over the rail, searching below for the saxophone player. He spit intermittently, just to watch it land.

Hallie peered over the opposite side. The water shimmered, silvery. She knew what her wish was now. Fishing the penny from the dark of her pocket, she flipped the coin over the edge, watched it fall. A long way down.

Crane perched himself on the rail and leaned out backward over the water. "Hey, Hallie!" he called to her.

"Crane! What are you— Hey, that's dangerous. You could fall."

"Look, no hands." Crane pretended he was about to let go.

"Don't! I mean it." She dashed to hold his hands firmly to the railing.

Crane laughed. "I was hoping I could get you to hold hands again." Hallie jerked her hands away. Her face burned.

He tilted back his head like a child on a roller coaster. "Ooooohhhh noooooo! Helllppp!" His voice stopped short. He straightened. "I think I see some-one up there," he told Hallie, nodding toward the arch of the bridge at the opposite end.

"You're just trying to get *me* to lean out there!"

"No, really. I can see the bottom of somebody's shoes dangling in the air. I'm not kidding! Look!"

"I can't see anything."

"Out here."

Hallie could not keep from looking down. The river no longer sparkled. Menacing now, the dark water rippled with dizzying effect. She imagined her-self falling, careening through the air. . . .

"Hallie? See him? Way up there. I'm sure it's a person. A strange man. Behind that cable."

Hallie righted herself on two rubbery legs. "Crane? Let's go home now."

"What? Now *that's* what I call dangerous. You

gotta be really crazy to climb up that high. How could he even get all the way up there? The guy must be half monkey! Heyyy!" Crane cupped one hand to his mouth and shouted.

"Crane, don't."

"C'mon. I don't think he hears us. We better go up to the top deck and say something to him. See if he's okay."

"No!" Hallie shouted. She wheeled sharply on one heel and fled down the sidewalk along the bridge. She scrambled back over the barricade, past the BRIDGE CLOSED sign, and broke into a run when she heard, "Hallie, wait up! I mean, what if he needs help or something?"

Somehow, before she had even looked up, before the red jacket caught her eye, Hallie knew. It was her father.

18

"Hallie, what's wrong? Are you sure you're okay?" Crane asked repeatedly on the bus ride home. Hallie held the secret inside her, tight as a clenched fist, until she left Crane and reached home.

"Mom! *Mom!*" she called, barely in the door, out of breath from running.

"Hallie, I'm right here. What? Did you have a good time?"

"Mom! It's Dad! I know it is. I mean, I knew it was him without even looking. Not just standing there on the deck like before. Up in the top, climbing around and everything!"

"Hallie, sit down and tell me. I can hardly understand a word you're saying."

"It's Dad, Mom! Out on the bridge. The Bridge to Nowhere. Crane and I, we walked over there. Crane saw him first. I mean, he didn't know it was Dad. Then, oh, Mom! I can't even . . . What is wrong with him? Something is wrong with him, Mom. People don't just . . . I'll never be able to face Crane again." She sank back on the couch, exhausted, having twisted the corners of a pillow into a pair of cat's ears.

Her mother was quiet for some time; then she reached over to smooth Hallie's hair away from her face. "Hallie, try not to think about it now. I'll speak to your father when he comes home. We'll work this all out. Don't worry, honey. This is not for you to worry over." Her voice trailed off. Hallie flipped on the television and stared. Anything to drive away the anger.

Neither of them spoke a word about her father's absence all during dinner. She dreaded his return, yet his empty place intruded on their silence.

Hallie was washing the dishes when her father barged into the kitchen. She felt his eyes boring a hole in her back. Reaching for the skillet, she saw that they were red-rimmed, bloodshot. He narrowed them to an accusing slit, squinting at her as if she were a criminal, then poured himself a drink. Hot tears formed at the back of her eyes. *Don't blink,* Hallie willed herself.

He sat down at his empty plate. Hallie scoured the skillet with a vengeance. Even with her back turned, she could hear the twirling. Unmistakably. The wedding ring.

"You missed dinner, Jim," her mother began gently.

"I had my dinner."

"How was the game?" her mother ventured.

"Fine."

"Who won—Cincinnati?" Hallie asked, challenging him.

"Pirates. Three to two, if you must know."

"Dad, it was four to one at the bottom of the ninth!"

"Maybe your father left Smitty's early, Hallie. Got something to eat, and the game wasn't over yet?"

"What is this, a test? First she asks the questions, then you?"

"Jim, I don't see why—"

"What I do in this house or anywhere else is my own business. I don't go snooping around in your business, and you don't go snooping around in mine."

"Jim, I . . . Something isn't right here. I think this *is* my business. When you say you're going somewhere, I at least expect—"

"Look, I'm sick and tired of being baby-sat! I just want to be left alone! Just once, would I like to be left alone!"

Hallie squeezed past her father's chair in an effort to make a quick exit. "Where are you going?" he said accusingly, grabbing hold of her wrist.

"Jim, let go of her. This is not—"

"Up to my room." Hallie wrenched her arm free.

Her father stood up, knocking back his chair. "Go ahead—run, like you always do!" he called after her.

"Jim, don't be so hard—"

"Like you did today!"

He saw me! Hallie thought indignantly, flinging herself on her bed in despair. On second thought, she marched out into the hallway and yelled down, "I should have called the police. The *police!*" Twice. Just to make sure he heard.

I'll tell Crane Monday, Hallie decided, *after school. I'll go over to the high school and find him and try to explain. Somehow.*

19

Hallie's conviction wavered as she wandered through the first floor of the high school, with people banging lockers, tossing books across the hall, shoving one another, and talking for the world to hear. The first person she asked had never heard of Crane. *I forgot, I should have asked about Monk. Maybe this isn't such a good idea after all,* she thought. *What am I going to say anyway?*

Hallie lingered, pretended to be reading a bulletin board until a guy with a gym bag knocked into her, nearly ran her over. "Hey, watch where you're going!" he called.

"Watch where *I'm* going," Hallie mumbled to herself.

He probably left school already, Hallie tried convincing herself, when she noticed an announcement for an upcoming meeting of the school newspaper. *Maybe that's where he'd be. If he stayed after.* Room 215, the sign said.

The door was closed. She looked to see if a meeting was taking place, but the room was empty. She turned the knob, tiptoed inside. "Crane?" she called. No answer, but music was blaring from the back corner. The door there said PHOTO LAB. A small sign read, THE PHOTOGRAPHER IS IN. PLEASE KNOCK. Hallie knocked, praying it *was* Crane on the other side of the door.

"Just a minute!" It sounded a little like his voice. The music quieted down; then the voice asked, "Who is it?"

"Crane, is that you?"

"Hallie? What are you doing here? Wait, hold on a second." In a few minutes, the door opened a crack. An arm reached out and pulled her inside. The room was dark except for a reddish cast that outlined everything with an eerie glow. "Sorry. I had to get these in the stop bath before I could let any light in."

"Developing pictures?"

"Yeah, I had a few rolls from . . ." Hallie couldn't blame Crane for his reluctance to mention the other day. "So, how'd you get here anyway? Stupid question—you walked, right? I mean, you know, how'd you find me? Oh, forget it. It doesn't matter. I'm just glad you did. I thought maybe you were mad at me or something. After the other day."

"Mad at you? Crane, I'm not mad at you."

"Well, you know, I thought maybe it was something I did or said or something. I don't know."

"Crane, I just . . ."

He looked at his watch. "Hold on again. I'm sorry—keep talking. I just have to time this while it's in the developer."

"Okay if I watch?" Hallie asked, welcoming the chance to change the subject.

"Sure. You can help. Come stand over here, and when I pass this to you, just dunk it in the one that says 'fixer.' "

With tongs, Crane was holding a sheet of shiny paper under some water in a small tub. He swirled it around and around, gently. Fuzzy gray patches appeared.

"Here. That's great, Hallie. Just keep moving it around. I'll tell you when."

"What is this stuff anyway?"

"Oh, just different chemicals, fixative and stuff. Don't get it on your clothes, though. Wear this." Crane handed her a long white lab coat like his.

"I feel like Dr. Frankenstein's assistant in this thing!"

"She's alive! Aliiiiive!" Crane held out both hands with crooked fingers in a monster impression.

Hallie laughed. "Hey, look, this is me! At the fountain the other day."

"A good one, too. When I pass this to you, hang it on the clothesline behind you to dry."

"You mean with these clothespins?"

"Yep. See, that's all there is to it. Now get ready for the next one."

"Hey, that one's me, too. How many pictures did you take?"

"This is the same shot. I'm just printing it a couple different ways. Some darker, some lighter. It's an experiment," Crane teased.

"Very scientific, Dr. Frankenstein."

"I can enlarge these, too."

"Oh, please. If this gets any bigger, you'll be able to count every hair on my head."

"I would like that."

"Gimme a break." Hallie wasn't quite sure how to respond to Crane sometimes.

Hallie and Crane worked side by side for a half hour, talking and joking together as easily as if they had been baking cookies in a brightly lit kitchen.

"Now, one more roll to develop." Crane handed Hallie a metal reel and showed her how to wind the film around it. "Practice a few times if you want, because this part you have to do in the dark."

"It's *already* dark in here."

"I mean all the way dark. HOOOOoooo!"

"How are you supposed to do this if you can't see, though?"

"By touch." Crane turned out the light. The room became darker than night. No shapes or shadows.

"Where are you?" Crane asked, groping in the darkness.

"Over here, Crane." He bumped into her.

"Hey, watch where you're going!" Hallie joked. "I've already been run over once today, in the hall."

"Okay, did you get the film out?"

"Yep. I'm just trying to find the slot it goes in." Hallie wound the film around the center of the reel as best she could without seeing. She wanted it to be right.

"Got it?"

"I think so. What do I do now?"

"Okay, now it goes inside that canister."

"I can't find it." They each patted their hands across the tabletop, searching.

"Here it is," Hallie announced. "But I can't get the lid off."

"Here, let me try." Crane put his hand on top of Hallie's. Instead of trying to twist off the lid, he held it there.

"Hallie, how would—" "Crane, I—" They both spoke at the same time.

"You first," Crane told her, still holding her hand. He was standing so close, she could smell his hair, like dark molasses. She thought it smelled good, but she didn't dare say so.

"Your hair smells good," Crane whispered, as if reading her thoughts. His breath tickled her ear. An unfamiliar quiver shot up through the center of her.

Hallie pulled away slightly. "About the other day, I—"

"Look, Hallie, before you say anything, don't feel that you have to explain. It's okay. Really."

"Well, I'm not sure how to . . . I mean, I don't know. I didn't mean to act weird. I guess just being out on the Bridge to Nowhere and seeing that man and everything. You see . . . my dad . . . well . . . "

"Shhh. Don't say any more."

Later, Hallie blamed it on the darkness. Once her sight had been taken away, all her other senses became sharper. Strangely keen. Alert. She could hear her own heart thumping, a drum without the drummer. Crane touched her hair tentatively, or was she mistaken? She heard him take in a quick breath, the tiniest gasp. Then she felt his lips, soft against her forehead, warm on her mouth.

Hallie did not know if she kissed him back. Her head was in a tailspin. She couldn't think. She started to cry. "Hhhh, hhhh, hhhh" was the only sound.

"Look, I'm sorry. Shhh. It's okay," Crane whispered, as if comforting a child. "Here, wait right there. Let me get the light."

"No!" Hallie protested. She had to get out of there. Fast. She could hardly stand. Like a gyroscope, her insides whirled in dizzy confusion, while her legs struggled to steady her. She groped blindly for the door, knocked over a glass bottle or beaker, heard it shatter in her wake. But she couldn't stop.

"Hallie, wait!" Crane was out the door after her. He reached and caught hold of her arm, pulling her back. "I didn't mean . . . You don't understand."

"No, *you* don't understand," she said between sobs. "Let me go!" *Running away. Again.*

And she was gone.

20

A knock on the door. "Hallie? Are you in there? It's Crane on the phone. Again."

"Mom, please. Tell him I'm asleep, tell him I'm at Jude's, I have homework, anything. Please?"

"Well, this is certainly a turnaround. What happened?"

"Mom, I can't explain about it. Just tell him not to call me anymore, okay?"

"I'll try. But I don't think it'll do any good. He seems very persistent."

"Mo-om," Hallie pleaded. She put a pillow over her head. Her mother left the room.

Shelley wouldn't have run, Hallie reproached herself. *Jude would've known exactly what to do. Maybe Dad was right about always running away. From him. From Crane. Two times! Like an idiot! First, because of Dad. Then, because of . . . What is wrong with me?*

She liked Crane—really liked him. And she wanted him to like her. But she hadn't expected . . . Hallie thought of her wish about Crane on the penny and shuddered.

It was only a kiss. If only she had stopped when he called after her. But he had grabbed her arm . . .

It had been dark. Pitch-black. She hadn't been able to see his face. It was so fast, she could hardly even remember how it happened, what it felt like. All she could remember was the darkness. And fleeing Crane, pushing him away. Then afterward, a sick feeling, her head spinning, her stomach doing flips as if she had just stepped off a ride at the amusement park.

At school, Jude leaned across the aisle in social studies and said, "You sure are acting strange lately. What is with you anyway?" Hallie shrugged her shoulders. She couldn't explain her confusion, even to her best friend—especially not in the middle of the Sudanese of Africa. Just when she was feeling comfortable with Crane, it had changed, like summer to fall in one day. One afternoon. One instant.

While she had once scanned the halls for Crane, sought him out, hoped for a chance meeting, she now avoided him, ducking around corners, slouching down into the seat on the bus. Until he started coming to her house.

The first time was Wednesday after school. Hallie didn't answer the knock. Instead, she tiptoed across the living room and peered from behind the curtains. Crane stood straight, arms stiff at his sides, as if on his best behavior. Hallie jerked away the second she spied him. Pressed her body to the wall. Stayed statue still, heart racing inside her chest.

She endured several minutes, hoping to hear his footsteps go back down the walk. When she dared a second glance, he was sitting patiently on the front stoop, idly shaving sticks with his penknife.

Now what should I do? Hallie thought. *When I don't show up, he'll know I was home the whole time. And what if Mom comes back? How long can he possibly wait there?* Stealthily, Hallie sneaked past the front door, up the stairs to her room. She could always pretend she'd been asleep. . . .

Three school days in a row, he came, sat, waited. Once he had gone, Hallie checked the front door, the milk box, the mailbox for a note, a sign. Nothing.

The following week, Hallie found herself under the dining room table, hiding. Just as she had spied Crane from her usual post, he moved toward the window, and she ran for cover. *Maybe I should just answer the door.* She owed him an explanation. *But what if he tries to kiss me again?*

Hallie thought about the homework she had to finish, but here she was, trapped, a prisoner in her own house. After what seemed like a half hour, she heard the storm door click open, then slam shut. *He must be leaving, finally!* Hallie crept from her hiding place, slinking around the corner in her stocking feet. No Crane. He'd given up. She felt an odd mixture of relief and disappointment.

21

"How did he do this? You never said he could carve."
Jude studied the small whittled whale, held it to the
light over the desk in her room. "Look how he got
the tail to curve up and everything. When did he give
you this?" Jude asked.

"Today. Well, he didn't give it to me, exactly. He
left it in the front door for me."

"Ooh, neat, a phantom caller. Boy, I bet you wished
you were home."

"That's just it. I was. I didn't answer the door."
Hallie tried unsuccessfully to explain to Jude about
hiding from Crane.

"You're nuts, Hal. Man, if it were me, I'd be waiting out on the front step. You wouldn't catch me
hiding from a guy who liked me that much."

"I know, I know. It's just now I don't know what to
do," Hallie agonized.

"Well, you could start by answering the door."

"I was thinking about it today. Really I was. But I
thought he left and it was too late. Then I heard
voices down in the garage. He must have realized

somebody was home, and now he's down there talking to my dad!"

"Probably just asking where you are."

"I know, but it's not like he just asked, then left. I mean, they've been together for a long time. Crane was still there when I sneaked over here."

"Hallie, you know he's just hanging around waiting to see you. You better go down there and say something."

"I can't, especially not now!"

"You're crazy, Hal. First you want him to like you, and you freak out when you think he likes Darlene. Then you hide whenever the guy comes over. Look, Hallie, I promised not to say anything, but Crane thinks you don't even *like* him."

"How do you know?"

"At band the other day, he was taking pictures. He was just about to shoot when he saw me and walked right up to ask if you were mad at him."

"I can't believe you wouldn't tell me. What else did he say?"

"He just thought you really liked him at first, but now he's worried that you don't, like maybe you changed your mind or something. He said you must really think he's a creep because you won't talk to him or anything."

"It's not that," Hallie said, avoiding any mention of the kiss. "I can't explain it. I'm not like you, Jude. I mean, you dance to records in the dark!"

"What's that got to do with anything?"

"Nothing. Never mind. It just gets me," Hallie said,

changing the subject. "I mean, what on earth could they be talking about all this time? The man barely talks as it is."

"Look, Hallie, if I were you, I'd march right down to that garage and straighten things out. You know, like you just got home or something. So what if your dad's down there."

"I guess. . . ." Hallie considered Jude's suggestion. "But I wouldn't know what to say. And you know my dad, Jude. He's like a chained dog."

"That's all you need—another dog bite!"

"Maybe Crane's left by now. Well, I'll think of something. Anyway, you're right. I can't be under house arrest forever."

"Be sure to let me know what happens," Jude said.

22

Belly-down on the den floor, Hallie put her ear to the heating duct. *He's still here!* She could hear the faint purr of conversation interspersed with the high-pitched whine of an electric drill. Upstairs, she opened the laundry chute, a tried-and-true trick of Shelley's. Never mind that her head once got stuck.

Crane's voice. "What's it like, though, working way up in the air like that all the time?"

Her father: "Nothing like it. When I'm on a job, walking the beams, looking down over the water, I'm on top of the world."

The good old days. In a way, she envied her father's oblivion, how he thought of nothing else, talked of nothing else but bridges—both envied and despised him for it at the same time.

Crane: "Don't you ever get scared that you're going to fall?"

You can't think about falling.

"Worst thing a man can do is think about falling. When you're up in the air, falling can't exist. At first, you're real shaky, looking down all the time, stomach getting kind of queasy. Pretty soon, you're not even laying planks anymore. Feels like you could do it blindfolded."

Hallie had heard descriptions of her father's feats as an ironworker a thousand times and had once been enamored, too. They had become tall tales for her, legends of an unsung hero—her father. The stories grew while the man faded.

What if he mentions the Bridge to Nowhere? she worried. *And what if Crane recognizes him? He couldn't have seen at that distance,* she reassured herself. Her two separate worlds had collided. She cracked her knuckles, tore at her nails as she listened some more.

The voices had subsided. *Crane must be gone.* She ran to the front window. No sign of him in the driveway, on the street. Then to the side window, overlooking the woods. Nothing. From the grating stop-start, stop-start of the grinder, Hallie concluded that her father had resumed his welding in the garage. She started downstairs.

"Dad?" Hallie asked, hesitantly at first, then "Dad!" to get his attention.

"What?" he answered from underneath his mask.

"Dad, was that Crane? I mean, was Crane over here?"

"Who?"

"Dad! You know perfectly well who!"

"Yeah, that was him."

She knew she was being unreasonable but asked anyhow, "Why didn't you call me?"

118

"Didn't think you were home," he answered flatly.

"Oh, Dad, you knew I was upstairs. I mean before."

"I did not *know* that."

"Well, what were you two doing down here anyway?"

"*I* was working on my sculpture. *He* was making a pest of himself, that's what. Asking a bunch of questions." Hallie couldn't see her father's eyes behind the dark goggles.

"Face it, Dad, you like having an audience," Hallie told him, bent on provoking. "I heard what you were saying, and Crane's too polite to tell you your bridge stories are boring."

"Anything else?" Without another word, her father picked up a hammer and flattened a strip of metal against the anvil.

"Dad, he's *my* friend!"

"Oh, so that's it. Well, don't look at me." He tipped the face shield up onto his forehead. "He's the one who came hanging around here asking a bunch of questions. I didn't invite him," her father spit out, as if the words left a bad taste in his mouth. The mask went down. He went back to pounding metal.

"I can't stand it anymore!" Hallie yelled, rage gushing out of her like water from a pipe that burst. "You don't care about me or anyone else. All you care about is that . . . that twisted . . . heap of metal. Excuse me . . . *sculpture*." She made the word sound sinister. "Even Mom says it's just a bunch of junk!"

"You think you know everything, Miss High-and-Mighty. Well, let me tell you—"

"Tell me what? Go ahead! You can't even come out from under that mask long enough to have a conversation with me, your own daughter!"

He lifted the mask but did not speak a word. The jagged lightning bolt of a scar over his lip whitened, flashing a warning signal. His eyes defied her to run.

She turned deliberately on her right heel and walked. Walked slowly toward the door to the basement, each step a statement.

"Hallie, come back here!" her father called harshly, as if reprimanding a disobedient dog. "You run away now and you're grounded!"

"Grounded! As if you'd notice. I could drop dead, and you wouldn't know the difference!" she shouted from the doorway.

"I mean it, Hallie!"

"I don't care what you mean, Dad. I don't care anymore. I just don't care." She slammed the door shut behind her so hard that it bounced back open, as if inviting one more angry insult.

"And why do you always have to wear that ugly old red jacket? Can't you change, just for once?" There. She'd said it. Screamed it. Finally. She knew now. She was sure of it. The red jacket had betrayed her. Crane must have seen it. Now he'd know about the weirdo on the bridge.

23

There was no thunderclap, no bad dream that awakened Hallie the next morning. No stopped clock that made her think twice. Nothing but the familiar knocking of pipes downstairs, on what appeared to be just another typical school day—until she saw Mrs. Spindler in the kitchen.

Mrs. Spindler was a spidery woman, with protruding purple veins and chin hairs, who had baby-sat for Hallie and Shelley when they were younger. Both girls called her Bette behind her back because she was scary-looking, like Bette Davis in the movies. "You girls better stop calling her that," their mother would warn, "because one day I'll forget her real name's Jeanette and call her Bette to her face!" The two girls had thought it a great joke.

Hallie was more puzzled than alarmed at first. She had not seen the woman for ages. Her parents had not gone out for so long. . . . "Mrs. S.! What are you doing here?" It was more an accusation than a simple question. Mrs. Spindler reached behind her ear to adjust her hearing aid. "Maybe she could hear if she'd ever stop clacking those knitting needles," the girls used to tell their mother.

"Just finishing up the dirty dishes, dear!" Mrs. Spindler answered, as if it were nothing out of the ordinary.

"Why are you here?" Hallie enunciated each syllable.

"I'm watching you, Henri honey." One of Mrs. Spindler's most infuriating habits was that she persisted in calling Hallie "Henri." To make matters worse, it often had a "honey" attached. It made Hallie feel like a stray cat.

"Mrs. S., I'm in seventh grade now. I think I'm old enough to stay by myself." Hallie heard the annoyance in her own voice. "Where's Mom anyway?" she tried again, in the impatient-trying-to-be-patient voice she had often heard her mother use.

"Henri honey, I am not supposed to upset you." She picked up her knitting, took a seat at the kitchen table. "Your mother called this morning. She said I should wait right here with you so that you would not be alone, and see that you don't go to school until she telephones us first thing."

"But I mean, where is she? Isn't she at work? Please, if you know something, just *tell* me, Mrs. Spindler." Hallie hated it when grown-ups upset her more by withholding information that might upset her.

Without looking up, Mrs. Spindler unraveled several stitches, resumed her knitting. "Your mother just said, 'Mrs. Spindler, I want you to—'"

"Where's my dad, then? Did he go, too?" Hallie interrupted before the woman recounted the entire conversation line by line.

"He's not here either, honey. Now we just have to wait."

"Wait for what? For somebody to talk to me? For somebody to tell me what's going on for once in my life? Why didn't Mom wake me up before she left? Nobody tells me anything!"

"Now, Henri, don't go getting yourself all worked up. Why don't you just go take a nice hot bath? Then you can fetch the morning paper, and we'll do the crossword. Take your mind off it while we wait for . . ." Mrs. Spindler was still talking, but Hallie's head swam. Swam with the empty chatter and persistent clatter of the knitting needles until she felt far, far away. Slowly, she backed out of the room.

Hallie had to be alone. Had to think. A knot tightened inside her chest, lodged at the base of her throat. What was so terrible that her mother couldn't tell her? Had she left in a hurry? What could she have been thinking, to leave her with a *baby*-sitter? Mrs. Spindler, the knitting nut. Mrs. Spindler, the crossword queen!

Hallie pulled on jeans and yanked a sweater over her pajama top. She had to move. Get out of the house. Walk. Jump on her bike. Anything. Keep moving. Anywhere.

But what if Mom calls?

"Is that you, Henri?" Mrs. Spindler called from the kitchen. *How is it that people who are near deaf when you're right on top of them can hear a door opening down the hall?* "Bring the paper in, dear." *Only Mrs. S. could think of crosswords at a time like this.*

Hallie bent to pick up the morning paper. The headline assaulted her.

ROSS MAN "FLIES" OFF BRIDGE TO NOWHERE

A grainy picture showed the wreckage of a station wagon turned upside down. Hallie read the caption:

It's a Long Way Down There
This car fell 100 feet, continued 90 feet forward.

A cold shudder went through Hallie. She felt her heartbeat rise to her throat.

A 100-foot plunge in an auto from the unfinished Fort Duquesne Bridge last night remains somewhat of a mystery. Forty-four-year-old James O'Shea of Ross Township pulled himself from the wreckage after his monumental flight across the Allegheny River, spanning 90 feet to the opposite shoreline. The auto was driven onto the span about 2:25 A.M. Tuesday, according to police.

"Daaaaad!" Hallie wailed, choking for air. Her eyes raced over the print.

Police said the high-flying former ironworker crashed through barriers at the downtown side and raced across the span of what is called "the Bridge to

Nowhere" because it ends high above the Allegheny River.

He broke through another barricade at the far side, flew through space, and landed upside down at the water's edge.

What! Broke through a barricade? Her heart slammed inside her chest. She couldn't make herself stop reading.

Officers estimated that Mr. O'Shea must have been traveling "at a tremendous rate of speed" to make the flying leap to land.

Nobody could . . .

Investigating Officer John S. Yard said sawhorses at the Point end of the bridge had been shoved aside and a cable, which had been attached to a guide by a turnbuckle, lay on the pavement.

"We didn't think it was possible to do anything like that," Yard said.

Oh, Daddy, please . . .

O'Shea was admitted to nearby Allegheny General Hospital, where he is reported to be suffering loss of memory.

No. No!
Hallie sat frozen, stunned. Cold all over. She refused to look at that picture again, but its indelible image burned in her mind's eye.

"James O'Shea," she said aloud, touching the words at the head of the column with her finger. "James O'Shea of Ross Township," she repeated in a daze, as if she had just heard the name for the first time, as if it did not belong to her own father.

The phone rang and Hallie jumped. She dropped the newspaper and ran to answer it, scattering the pages to the floor, facedown.

24

Her mother cried, then struggled to keep her voice even. That was all Hallie heard at first, the crying. The words themselves were not making any sense. Words made it sound acceptable for her father to be in the hospital, as if he had nothing but a broken leg or a smashed finger.

"He drove off a bridge, Mom!" Hallie screamed. Mrs. Spindler paced the floor now, wringing the dishtowel until the knobs of her knuckles turned white, her face ghostly pale. She began madly putting away dishes.

When Hallie said, "I want to come see Daddy," her mother instructed her, "Stay right where you are, Hallie. I'll call you back in a few hours. Daddy can't have visitors yet. He can't talk to anybody right now."

"What's going to happen, Mom? I mean, is he going to be all right?"

"He'll be fine," her mother reassured her. "He's all one now, honey. I have to go."

"What? 'All one'?" Hallie thought she meant to say "alone" but wasn't quite sure. "Wait, Mom . . ."

"Hallie, have Mrs. Spindler stay there with you so you're not alone, too, okay? I'll try to reach Shelley at school this afternoon. You just sit tight. Don't worry about school. Everything's going to be okay. I promise. I'll talk to you later." *Zzzzzzzz*. Dial tone.

How can she promise? Hallie wondered. She had to see her father. Make sure. She couldn't wait. It would be hours before her mother called back, before she would know anything. She had to apologize. Say she was sorry. Tell him she didn't mean those things.

Hallie collapsed into the first empty seat she could find. Her head felt too heavy for her shoulders. She propped it against the bus window, shut her eyes. It rattled and jolted, giving her a fierce headache, but she didn't move. When she arrived at the hospital after running several blocks through the North Side, she had only a vague recollection of getting there. Cars honked, lights changed, people hurried to their destinations, but to Hallie the world had stopped cold. Yet no one took notice of her. No one knew that the man on the front page was her father.

Inside, a nurse asked her where she was going. Why wasn't she in school? She would have to wait. She wasn't old enough. She must be accompanied by an adult—hospital policy. Where was her mother?

Hallie kept unsticking her legs from the vinyl chair in the waiting room. Her stomach felt hard and hollow at the same time. She watched her tennis shoe shake rapidly back and forth, but her own foot felt far away.

Her mother would be furious when they informed her that she was in the waiting room on her father's floor. But Hallie was angry, too. Why couldn't she see her own father? What did they think she was going to do, pop her gum too loud?

She waited for the man in the gray jacket at the volunteer desk to call her name. To say that her mother was coming to meet her. That she could go see her father now. To tell her he was doing just fine.

Across from her, a lady with fat ankles stole glances at her watch, nervously flicked ashes on the carpet. Hallie watched them land. *Ashes, ashes, we all fall down.* The phone rang, startling her. *Be for me,* she prayed silently. "Mrs. DeRisio," the man in the gray jacket called, adding what sounded like one too many syllables. The lady squinted one eye and took a long last draw on her cigarette, crushing it over and over in the ashtray, as if stalling for time. *Okay, it's out!* Hallie felt like shouting. The woman left, her heels clicking in reprimand against the quiet corridor.

Hallie went back to biting her nails down to the quick. She wanted to feel them sting.

In her restlessness, she picked up a magazine from the table. SEVEN STEPS TO A HEALTHIER YOU. *Please be all right, Dad.* DON'T FIGHT IT . . . FIRM IT! *Oh, Daddy, please. Why did you have to do this?* HOW TO TALK SO KIDS WILL LISTEN. *I won't fight any-more. Cross my heart and hope to . . . From now on. Just be okay.* She worked on biting the inside of her lip. *Please, God, don't let anything bad happen. Make him be okay.*

It's funny about praying, Hallie thought. *You forget all about God for the longest time, then something bad happens, and there you are talking to somebody invisible, asking for things, pleading, making promises.*

Hallie didn't care. She promised never to get mad at her father again. What made him drive off a bridge? Was it all those terrible things she had said? Why did she say them anyway? Had he been planning this all along, during all those trips to the bridge? Had he been trying to kill himself? *Don't think that. Think something else. Anything. Two times two is four. Four times four is eight. No, sixteen. Humpty-Dumpty sat on a wall, Humpty-Dumpty had a great fall. Hail Mary, full of grace. . . .*

She opened her eyes. The room was too bright. Fluorescent white. It smelled like adhesive tape. She needed air—real air, not this ventilated kind. Tried the window. No handle. Fake. She moved away from the blower. Shivered. Hugged her arms to herself. Closed her eyes again. Tried to conjure up the woods, the smell of warm leaves . . . no use. Nothing to do but wait. Memorize the dirt spots on the carpet.

Where was her father's room anyway? Fifth floor. Wasn't five an unlucky number? *Oh well, could have been worse. Could have been thirteen.* Hallie had heard once that there wasn't a thirteenth floor in buildings like hotels, because people were too superstitious to stay there. *How can they do that?* she wondered. *Just skip a whole floor? Besides, wouldn't the fourteenth floor really be the thirteenth? Did they ever think of that?*

Silence. The phone refused to ring, the way a watched-for shooting star is never there.

I should have brought something for Dad, Hallie thought. *Something to give him, for his room.* Hallie remembered falling off her swing set when she was five and hitting her head. Her father had come home in the middle of the day and brought her a hard hat, her very own, blue, with her name printed across the front.

She thought of Shelley. *How's she going to feel, not being here?* She thought of Crane, too. Would he ever want to be her friend again? Probably not now. Not only would he know about the day at the bridge . . .

Don't cry. She picked up another magazine. *Not here.*

Footsteps. She saw her mother heading toward her. Hallie managed to stand, even though her feet seemed rooted to the floor. "I thought I told you to stay put" were her mother's angry first words, but Hallie hardly heard them. Just seeing her mother made her burst into tears. "Honey, honey . . ."

She felt only the scratchy wool of her mother's blazer rubbing against her face.

25

"Daddy can't remember things, honey. The doctor says it will be too confusing to see people," Hallie's mother said, over the clatter of cafeteria trays.

"But, Mom, it's not like I'm—"

"Hallie. I do not want an argument about this. You're pushing your luck just being here right now. As soon as I check on your father once more, I am taking you home. Period."

Hallie was silent, thinking. Then suddenly: "Mom, I left my jacket upstairs!"

"Well, go phone Mrs. Spindler first. That woman must be worried sick. I'll meet you up on the fifth floor in ten minutes. I want to pick out a magazine or a book for Dad."

"You mean he can read?"

"Yes, he can read. Take this change for the phone."

Ten minutes. Barely enough time. Hallie made her call in a hurry, then took the elevator up to six, just in case. When she found the back stairs, she sneaked down one flight, carefully opened the door into the hall, and tiptoed more softly than Santa Claus. She had seen her mother coming from this wing. Ritzel, Kastal, Mancuso. Hallie scrutinized the names outside each door. Letteri, Callahan, Kowalsky, O'Shea. O'Shea!

She heard voices. A curtain was half-drawn around her father's bed. All she could see of him were his hands. Work hands, creased with dirt, resting in their own handshake against the starched sheet.

"Your home address, Mr. O'Shea," a man's voice said in a foreign accent. "Do you know where you live?" *Of course he knows where he lives,* Hallie thought. "Two twenty-two Mary Vue Road," she heard her father answer.

"I understand you have two daughters?"

"Yes."

"Can you tell me their names?"

"Shelley and Hallie."

"Full names?"

"Shelley Lynn and Henrietta Elizabeth. After her grandmother," her father added.

"Dates of birth?"

"June and September. I don't remember the exact dates. But I don't think I'd remember anyway."

Oh, Dad! Don't say that! Hallie thought.

"So you weren't certain of these dates before the accident, Mr. O'Shea—is that correct?" The doctor sounded disapproving.

The accident? How do you accidentally drive off a bridge?

"For pete's sake, Doc, I'm not really sure."

Pause. The doctor must have been marking his chart. "Mr. O'Shea, if you had two quarters, three dimes, and a nickel, what would you have?"

What does that have to do with anything? Hallie thought.

"A pocketful of change," her father said sarcastically.

"Mr. O'Shea, I know these questions may seem elementary, but we must try to establish the nature of your amnesia."

"Okay, okay. Eighty-five cents."

Go, Dad!

"If you had to ride a bus, Mr. O'Shea, where would you buy a ticket?"

"You mean if I didn't have the change? I guess I'd go to the bus station, or a drugstore might sell tickets."

"What kind of car were you driving last night, Mr. O'Shea?"

"I don't know."

"No idea?"

"None."

"Do you remember where you were going when you left your house last evening?"

"I don't remember a thing."

"The store? A bar? To meet a friend? Try to think, Mr. O'Shea. This is very important. Try to get a picture, an image in your mind."

"Look, we've been all over this before. I'd like to help you out, Doctor. Really I would. But it's just a big blank. . . ."

Hallie couldn't stay to hear more. She hurried back to the waiting room before her mother returned, praying she wouldn't notice that Hallie had no jacket. Hallie picked up a magazine and propped it open in her lap, as if GREAT BUYS FOR GUYS were now the most interesting article in the world.

26

Hallie had hoped to visit her father once Shelley came home, but Shelley never even mentioned going to the hospital. It seemed to annoy her that she'd been called away from college. *He could have died!* Hallie wanted to say to her, impress upon her, but she kept quiet.

Shelley spent most of her time studying in her room with the door shut. "Hurry up in the bathroom!" or "Why do you always leave the light on?" was the extent of conversation with her. When Hallie tried to draw her out, Shelley's response was, "Hallie, I have to read three hundred fifty pages, finish a take-home exam, and write two papers by next Tuesday."

"Why are you so mad all the time?" Hallie finally asked.

"Hallie, you just don't get it, do you? Never mind."

"Get what? I mean, just 'cause you have a lot of homework."

"Hallie, I'm in college, in case you hadn't noticed."

"Yeah, and Dad's in the hospital."

"Yeah? So what. Maybe he should have thought of that before he went and drove off a bridge!"

"Don't you even *care*? All you care about is stupid college."

"Oh, and you think *he* cares? You are really thick, you know that? Dad cares about one thing—himself."

"I tried to tell you, Shelley. *You're* the one who said nothing was wrong."

"Oh, fine. Blame me. Okay, it's *my* fault Dad tried to kill himself. I should have been here to stop him from flying off some bridge in the middle of the night at ninety miles an hour!"

"Shut up, Shelley! You don't know! You don't know anything!" Hallie marched into the next room and slammed the door defiantly. Shelley slammed her own door, as if to have the last word.

Hallie threw herself facedown on her bed and cried until her throat throbbed. The anger washed away. One thought haunted her. *Why would Dad want to stop living?* She had been careful not to let herself think that. She refused to believe it. But Shelley made it sound so true.

If only Dad could come home, Hallie thought. *But what if he'll never be the same again?* All those times she had hated him, wished him away. Now she missed him. Had he been gone for months, or was this only the second day? *Will he even know who I am? What would I say to him?* she worried. *What if Shelley's right? Maybe he just doesn't care.*

Hallie wiped her eyes with her sleeve. She remembered crying as a little girl, cradled in her father's lap. What had she cried about then? He would pull a handkerchief with a monkey face embroidered on it from his pocket. The monkey was always frowning. "Monkey is sad," her father would say. Then he'd turn it upside down, and it became a clown with a big smile. Like magic.

The memory drew Hallie down the dusky hall into her parents' silent room. She cautiously pulled the handles on the top drawer of her father's tall dresser, eased them back quietly so they would not clink. Inside were mounds of dark socks snuggled into round balls. A pile of soft, unironed handkerchiefs. Hallie picked one up, rubbed it against her cheek, smelled it. A box of Q-tips, his best tie, a small blue penknife. When she unfolded the blade, it made a tiny pair of scissors. Some foreign coins. Her father's watch. *Why wouldn't Daddy have his watch with him?*

Way in back, she pulled out a stack of dog-eared papers rubber-banded together. On top was an old report card: Shelley O'Shea, St. Scholastica, Grade 8. All M's. Marked progress was the highest grade. To MY VALENTINE. Hallie recognized her own large printing on a card she had made in elementary school. There were hearts cut out of white doilies, red construction paper glued in back. Each heart said DADDY in the middle. *I can't believe he saved this stuff!* She unfolded a piece of notebook paper. A poem began:

Mary's three
She broke her doll
It isn't much
To her it's all
That's sorrow

Hallie O'Shea. Grade 3.

Where did Dad even get these things? A smashed tissue-paper flower, a favorite quote that Shelley had lettered in calligraphy, a school picture from kindergarten when Hallie looked like a boy. *He saved them all this time!*

Suddenly Hallie felt like an intruder. She bundled the cards and papers back together, tucking them behind the socks gingerly, as if they might break or crumble.

Back in her own room, she turned on the light. She thought about Shelley, and about facing school tomorrow. Everyone would know.

It dawned on her then that she had not found what she started out looking for—the monkey handkerchief. Instead, she found a forgotten poem, a hidden valentine, an unremembered photograph that each told her something about her father. The discovery grew inside her like a secret. It was already beginning to shape itself into something new, a pearl from sand.

27

"Amnesia," Hallie told Jude on the way to school Thursday.

Jude was all questions. "*Amnesia?* Amnesia like he can't remember his name or anything?"

"He remembers some stuff, like who the president is, but not anything about what happened."

"Well, what about . . . Is he hurt?"

"Just some cuts and scrapes, really, but they're keeping him in the hospital. For observation, Mom says."

"Oh, Hallie, it's awful. But at least he's pretty much okay. I mean, does he recognize you?"

"I don't know. He hasn't seen me yet." She was glad when they neared her locker, because she didn't feel much like talking.

Hallie stopped short.

"Oh no," Jude said, covering her mouth.

A bumper sticker was stuck to the outside of Hallie's locker. In fluorescent orange letters, it read:

Enter the
Cordic and Company
BRIDGE LEAP CONTEST

"I can't believe it! Some people are really sick. Sometimes I hate this place," Jude said, outraged. A bell rang for homeroom. "How did they even get hold of one that fast?"

"I don't get it. What does it mean?" Hallie asked her.

"Oh, Hal, I was hoping you wouldn't have to hear about this. See, Rege Cordic, the radio announcer from KDKA, saw the headlines about your dad. Well, when it seemed that he wasn't hurt bad, he made this thing up for a joke, called the Bridge Leap Contest. It's not real or anything. It's just bumper stickers, and people are supposed to put them in funny places." Jude said the words really fast.

"But it's not funny. It's not funny one bit! He's not okay. He could have died! And he's still in the hospital!" Hallie fled down the hall straight for the girls' bathroom.

Jude chased after her. "Hallie? *I* didn't mean it was funny. I was just trying to explain."

"I know, I know. I'm sorry. It's just that it's so mean. How am I going to get that thing off?"

"Right now, you're going to be late for homeroom."

"I don't care. You go ahead. I have to stay here for a few minutes."

"Are you sure?"

Hallie nodded.

"Okay. . . . I'm glad you're back, Hal. Really I am."

Hallie sat inside a stall with the door locked until the first-period bell rang and snapped her back to reality. She splashed cold water on her face and walked to English the long way around. *Not* past her locker.

When she reached the classroom, Miss Sands was at the door. "Welcome back, Hallie," her teacher said. As she took her seat, Hallie felt like a new student, the way everyone stared at her. And Miss Sands had never before called her Hallie.

All day long, everyone treated her as if she had some strange disease. "I'm not sick!" she felt like shouting. The hours seemed unending. She had never been so relieved to hear the final bell. But she could no longer avoid going back to her locker.

Someone had taken a knife and scraped off the bumper sticker! Only traces of the paper backing stuck to the door. *Thank you,* Hallie silently whispered, *whoever you are.*

A note was wedged into the door of her locker, barely visible. HALLIE! THIS IS A TREASURE HUNT. FOLLOW THE CLUES. Hallie recognized the crooked handwriting and couldn't help smiling. She opened the first clue.

IN A ROOM FILLED WITH NOTES,
SOMEONE ONCE WROTE.

Hmm. *A room filled with notes.* Sometimes people stuck notes on the bulletin board, but almost every room had one of those. Maybe it meant the office. No. How could anyone hide something there? Then she thought of it. *The music room!*

After scouring the room for another written note, she noticed musical notation on the board. Like a code, she deciphered the letter for each one. F-E-E-D-F-A-C-E. Feed face? *Feed face! The cafeteria!*

The hunt continued until, after three more clues, Hallie found herself on the stage in the auditorium. She was searching all around the piano, feeling foolish, when Crane stepped out from behind the curtain. "Looking for something?" he asked, his eyes sparkling.

"Yes, as a matter of fact. But what I'm looking for is very hard to find. See, I don't know what it looks like," Hallie teased.

"I see," Crane said, pretending to sound serious. "So you're looking for something, you know not what, but you think it may be in the piano? Is that it?"

"Something like that."

There was a long pause. Then they both spoke at once. "Hallie, I heard about . . ." "Crane, I'm sorry I . . ." They laughed.

"You first," Crane said.

"I'm sorry how I acted. I don't know why. . . . It was really stupid."

"No, I'm sorry. Really. I heard about your dad and everything. I wanted to call you, but I wasn't sure. I mean, I was hoping you'd be back yesterday, then today. . . ."

"Oh, Crane . . ." Tears welled in Hallie's eyes.

143

Then they were hugging, hard. When Hallie opened her eyes, she saw only the dark, velvety curtains of the stage, a backdrop like night.

"I think I made you miss your bus," Crane said. "But I'm glad you found me."

"Me, too."

28

Hallie ran into the living room when she heard the crash of the metal rod.

"Mom, what's . . . ? Are you all right?"

Her mother had been taking down curtains, washing windows. "He's coming home, Hallie. Your father. They're releasing him today!" Her eyes filled with tears.

"That's great, Mom. I can't believe it. It's only Sunday. I thought they were keeping him. . . . Then it must mean he's okay, there's nothing wrong with him. If they're letting him out and everything."

With barely a nod, her mother asked suddenly, "How do the windows look?" Not waiting for an answer, she went on: "I think I'll make a nice roast before I leave for the hospital."

"Will he know us, Mom? Do you think he'll know who we are? I mean, Jude says . . ."

"Of course he'll know you, honey. He just can't remember the accident, that's all. Can you run and get the vacuum, Hallie?"

The accident. There it was, that word again. Even Mom was calling it that now.

"Mom, I think Dad's seen a dirty house before," Shelley remarked from the doorway. "I've never known him to give it the white-glove test."

"I know. I just want everything to be perfect," she said, steepling both hands in a gesture of prayer.

He returned, ushered in through the front door, a guest in his own house. Hallie took the stairs singly, noiselessly, hesitating on the bottom landing. She had imagined a more dramatic entrance: racing down the steps, collapsing in his arms, crying, convincing him she was sorry. So terribly sorry.

Her father walked around the room as if seeing it for the first time. He ran his fingers along the edge of a fuzzy cactus on the windowsill, stepped over to the mantel and stood on the hearth. "Those are the cards people sent, the ones I was telling you about," her mother said nervously. "I hope it was okay . . ." Her voice trailed off. Her father picked up a framed picture, touching the faces there through the glass. He held it closer, studying it, trying to discern something he had perhaps never noticed.

"Oh, Jim," her mother said shyly. "It's good to have you back."

"It's good to be here, Louise." He turned and hugged her, spotting Hallie over her mother's shoulder.

Hallie watched her father walk across the room in slow motion, felt his arms around her, his chin resting on her head. "I didn't see you there," her father told her. Then he held her at arm's length. "You must have grown an inch."

"Dad, you've been gone only five days." Hallie laughed.

"Six, counting today. Seems longer."

He hugged her again. She could hear his heartbeat. "Where have you been?" she heard him whisper.

"Oh, Daddy, I wanted to come see you. I tried . . ." She was crying now.

"I know, honey. I know. Your mother told me. It's okay." After a minute, he took his thumbs and dabbed the corners of Hallie's eyes, trying to catch the tears as they spilled over.

"I thought you said Shelley was home." He raised an eyebrow in her mother's direction.

"She is. Upstairs. I guess she didn't hear us come in. She has an enormous amount of schoolwork."

"Maybe I better go up." He took off his jacket, a green one. Hung it in the hall closet.

"Help me get the table set, Hallie." Hallie listened to him knock on the door upstairs before going into the kitchen with her mother.

Twenty minutes passed. No Shelley. "I hate to yell up for dinner. We'll just have to keep things on low," her mother said.

"What smells so good?" her father asked, entering the kitchen. "Mmm. A home-cooked meal. I've had enough Jell-O to last me a lifetime!"

"Jim, you sit there." Hallie's mother pointed to his regular place. "Hallie, go call your sister."

"Better leave her be, Hallie," her father cautioned.

Her mother furrowed her brow. "The food will get cold."

He twisted his wedding ring out to the end of his finger, paused, pushed it back on. "It'll wait. She'll be down when she's ready," he answered. "Let's go ahead and eat. I'm starving."

Shelley finally made an appearance at the end of the meal, her eyes red-rimmed and puffy. Their mother leaped from her chair. "There's plenty of roast, Shelley. Let me warm it up."

"Yeah, but I ate all the potato pancakes," Hallie confessed.

"No, I put two away."

Shelley sat down. "Dad, I've decided to take you up on your offer."

"What offer?" their mother asked.

"Shelley's reading *Our Mutual Friend*," their father said.

"Oh, I used to love Dickens in college."

"Not when it's over a thousand pages long, you wouldn't," Shelley complained.

"So I told her if she filled me in on the characters, I could pick up where she left off and read a couple of hundred pages for her, let her know what happens."

"I see," their mother said, smiling.

"You'll have to read the ending yourself, though." He held out his hand. "Deal?"

"Deal," Shelley answered, shaking it.

29

"I'm worried about him, Kay," Hallie heard her mother say on the phone one evening. "He seems cheerful enough when he's up, but he hardly moves off that couch. I'm afraid maybe he does have a head injury."

Shelley had gone back to school, with the final chapter of Dickens still ahead of her. A hush had fallen over the house—perhaps a sigh, suspended in midair, or the weight of unasked questions. Hallie wasn't quite sure what to talk about with her father, but suddenly they'd laugh, easily, as if nothing had ever happened.

After dinner one night, he said, "Louise, where are the keys to your car?" Her mother stiffened at the question. Hallie nearly tipped over a glass of milk, rescuing it in the nick of time.

"Everyone relax. I'm just going to the hardware store. I'll be back in a half hour. An hour, tops."

"Jim, do you really think you should be driving so soon after . . . ?" She did not say "the accident" but apparently could find no other word.

Neither of them knew why he suddenly decided to go to the hardware store. "I'll do the dishes tonight, Hallie," her mother told her. In the time her father was gone, her mother not only washed the dishes but scrubbed the counters, wiped down the stove, and mopped the floor. "I think I heard a car," she said once, hurrying to carry the trash downstairs.

They didn't know what he bought that night, if he purchased anything. They didn't dare ask. But after the car pulled in and the garage door closed, her mother stopped her cleaning frenzy and sat down. Hallie could hear her father puttering in the basement, running water, whistling to himself. "What that man is up to now, I can't guess." Her mother sighed.

"At least he's not lying on the couch," Hallie said, sighing herself.

The next day when Hallie came home from school, she found her father in the kitchen. It was a mess. Her mother's clean kitchen! There were torn sheets all over the floor, contents of cabinets strewn everywhere, newspaper in shreds on counters and table.

"Dad! What are you doing up there?"

From the top step of the ladder, he said, "I know, I know. I'm the last guy who should be up this high, right?"

"No, really."

"Painting the kitchen—what does it look like?" he teased.

"You mean just like that? You're painting the kitchen?"

"I thought your mother might like a yellow kitchen."

"But you said you hated taking down old wallpaper!"

"Not as much as I hate reading Dickens! But that's just between you and me, okay? Of course your mother's probably going to have a fit. Look at this place. And I've got only one wall done. Maybe when I tell her we have to eat out tonight, she'll forgive me. . . . Think so?"

Light was streaming in the window, filling every corner and crack. "Well, it does seem a lot brighter in here," Hallie said.

"Just wait till I strip the cabinets, too. They'll be much lighter and—"

"Dad, I think I hear water running downstairs."

"Look out back." He nodded toward the window.

Hallie peered out over the kitchen sink. "Hey, what's that, your sculpture?"

"I decided it's finished. I'm calling it The River. What do you think?"

"The River," Hallie pondered, trying it out. "I see it now, Dad. I really do. Before I thought it was a snake or something." Hallie laughed. "It looks different now. Like a fountain. With the water, I mean." Water swirled and curved in spiral streams, then flowed to the next level. A halo of fine mist shrouded the sculpture, catching the light in places. "All those tiny rainbows. How did you get the water to do that?"

"It came to me lying in that hospital bed. Staring at the same picture on the wall all day. Not remembering. Then I thought of it. Drilling tiny holes in a circular pattern to create that effect. I still have to hook up a pump, but for now I ran a hose out to it. Just to see."

Hallie turned from the window, faced her father. "Were you afraid? Not remembering anything? And everybody else knowing?"

"I was plenty scared at first. Not of them—of me. Something inside me. Oh, I saw the stares, heard the whispers, imagined all the things people were saying."

"It was just a big blank?"

"That's exactly what I told the doctor. I racked my brain trying to remember something. Anything. Like waking up out of a deep sleep. You're sure you were dreaming, your heart's even beating fast, but you can't remember what the dream was about."

"You're not afraid anymore?"

"I got to thinking, Hallie. Realized I was lucky. To be able to choose, make up my own mind. Right then's when I decided to paint this kitchen. Yellow. Isn't that funny? It popped into my head out of nowhere, just like that."

Hallie looked around the room, at the unfinished white plaster walls. "Hey, Dad," Hallie said, forming an idea. "As long as you're going to paint this . . ." She drew out the words.

"Yes?"

"Could I, you know, maybe write on the wall? Or draw something? I mean, you're just going to paint over it anyway, right?"

"Be my guest, Picasso. We've got markers, brushes, rollers. . . . Here, hold out your hands," he said, "and close your eyes."

Hallie held out both hands, palms open toward her father. She could tell he placed a pen in one. "Keep your eyes closed," he warned. Something wet and slippery was in the other.

"Hey, no fair!" she said, opening her eyes, but she was laughing at her yellow hand, fingers oozing with fresh paint. "Let *me* have that brush."

"Sorry, I need it," her father said, indicating the job before him.

Hallie pressed her palm against the wall, leaving a perfect handprint.

"Hey, Dad," she said, wiping the rest of the yellow on a rag. "I was telling Crane about when we used to have that parakeet in here. And you would call up the operator, remember?"

"Yep."

"You really do?"

"Of course I do. Buddy. You and Shelley named him."

Her father continued painting. Hallie stared at the blank wall in front of her, like a chalkboard erased clean, except for the handprint. She puzzled over what to make of it.

Tentatively, she held the pen to the wall. She began with small letters:

HALLIE WAS HERE.

I I I I I NO ONE SUSPECTS, so many years later, that this was once the Bridge to Nowhere.

The bridge spans the distance now, stretching from riverbank to riverbank, a shiny sentinel amid skyscrapers. No longer silent, it creaks and groans with its own weight. People going and coming, coming and going. The steady thrummm of traffic, the thunk thunk of cars and trucks over the steel grating drown out any other possibilities of sound.

They do not stop. They do not see. They do not hear. They do not remember.

But if you pause, you can still smell the river, pungent with wet leaves newly fallen, witness a family of sea gulls swooping low, or tugs gliding past, each one pushing a line of barges. If you look closely, you may detect traces of graffiti from another time bleeding through. Listen carefully. Can you hear it? No more than a whisper.

Notes from a saxophone? Voices? Perhaps the distant voices of bridge builders, you say. Then you remember.

I I I I I I I I I